PADDY NO MORE

PADDY NO MORE

Modern Irish Short Stories

Edited by WILLIAM VORM

Wolfhound Press

Published 1978 by WOLFHOUND PRESS,
98 Ardilaun, Portmarnock,
County Dublin

ISBN 0 905473 28 0 (Cloth)

First published in USA 1977 by Longship Press

Printed in the Republic of Ireland

FOR THREE YOUNG READERS
Erik, Francis, and Diana

Acknowledgments

The following material has previously appeared in the publications shown. ATLANTIS: *The Stormy Petrel* by Francis Stuart. CHICAGO REVIEW: *Hemisphere* by Juanita Casey. COMHAR: *The Blessed Wagtail* by Eoghan Ó Tuairisc. THE HONEST ULSTERMAN: *The Humours of Ballyturdeen* and *O'Fuzz* by John Morrow. NEW IRISH WRITING (THE IRISH PRESS): *The Well* by Juanita Casey, *Per Ominy Ah* by Eoghan Ó Tuairisc, *Transients* and *The Shaking Trees* by Lucile Redmond. SOUNDINGS: *The Stranger* by Michael Foley.
Death of a Chieftain is from the collection "Death of a Chieftain and Other Stories" published by MacGibbon and Kee.
Permission to reprint the article *The Soft Centre of Irish Writing* has been granted by The Irish Times.

Contents

Illustrations

Foreword *by William Vorm*

This book came about as the result of nearly six months spent in Ireland last fall and winter, reading as much as possible, and talking to writers and others with a considerable knowledge of current Irish literary efforts. I have tried to assemble stories by writers who are in various, and often dissimilar, ways trying to get away from the traditional style of the Irish short story, however cozy, and often well written, it may be. Hence the title *Paddy No More*.

The concern about the direction of Irish literature felt by many writers is vigorously presented in an article by the novelist Francis Stuart, *The Soft Centre of Irish Writing*, that appeared in the Irish Times in October, 1976. I am including this important and timely piece in *Paddy No More*, in a sense to set the stage for the short stories that follow. This is not to say that Mr. Stuart is the spokesman for any group, or 'school of writing.' He is very much his own man, and always has been.

The writers represented are of all ages– the younger half in their late twenties, including members of the Irish Writers' Cooperative, a group that publishes its own work. Two are very non-staid members of the Irish Academy of Letters (Montague and Stuart). Some have received Hennessy Literary Awards, Irish-American Cultural Institute Awards, or Bursaries from the two Arts Councils (Republic of Ireland, and Northern Ireland). Most of the stories have previously appeared in print, generally with a somewhat restricted circulation, and I am grateful to have received permission to use them. About a third have not been published before, and, to my knowledge, only one has been published in the United States.

I have included four writers who identify themselves as 'Northerners,' from Ulster; Michael Foley, John Morrow, John Montague, and Francis Stuart. There is a very strong literary tradition in the North, toughened and intensified, no doubt, by the bloody war which has raged in Ulster since 1970, claiming nearly two thousand dead.

Several of the stories touch on the North; the two black humor tales of John Morrow meet aspects of this conflict head on, and John Montague's story views Ulster from another angle.

I have retained the authors' original spelling, and have not Americanized any of the words used in their stories. I hope this will not cause any reader inconvenience.

I want to thank some of those who have helped me find material for this book: Michael Longley of the Arts Council of Northern Ireland, David Collins of An Chomhairle Ealaion (the Irish Arts Council), and David Marcus of the Irish Press. In 1968, Mr. Marcus started the weekly New Irish Writing page, a platform for the work of Irish writers, recognized and unknown. He also initiated the annual Hennessy Literary Awards (1971) for new and developing writers which appeared in the page.

Above all, I must thank the individual writers who gave so much of their time and thought, and enthusiastically and unhesitatingly led me to other writers I might have overlooked.

An Afterthought

'Short stories don't sell!' I was cautioned by presumably knowledgeable members of a couple of large publishing houses, by a literary agent, and even by a bookstore owner. I am not persuaded of the truth of this old saw. I think that, particularly in our harried times, someone interested in good reading would derive greater satisfaction from an hour or so spent with a pertinent, well constructed, short story, rather than confronting the inevitable and omnipresent megatome, whatever its merit. Just for a change. A good number of ordinary book readers (and a few book dealers) I have discussed this with agree– there aren't too many short stories available, in book form.

Another thing: how can the short story writer reach a wider audience than that of the literary magazine (other than by means of the very occasional sale to a mass circulation periodical) if book publishers decide by *fiat* that the short story is of no interest? I obviously don't share this opinion, and if I find, as I hope, that *Paddy No More* is viable financially, I plan to publish similar collections from other countries.

Publisher's Note

William Vorm who selected and edited this collection of modern Irish short stories is publisher of the Longship Press in the United States of America.
The 'Foreword' above, from the American edition (Longship Press, 1977) of this collection, explaining the concept 'Paddy No More' of the title and expressing confidence and hope for contemporary Irish writing and for the short story, has been retained unaltered in this edition.

FRANCIS STUART

The Soft Centre of Irish Writing

1976

WE ONCE had some remarkable writers in our land. Yeats, Joyce, Flann O'Brien and Patrick Kavanagh make up no mean tally for so small an island. None of these, with the possible exception of Yeats, made much impact on their society. The writers who influenced this community, and were readily taken to its heart, were those who reflected, more flatteringly, its habits and thought-modes.

The relation of the imaginative artist to his society is important for both. If the truly original artist is ignored or rejected he is driven into an isolation from which his best work may spring, and the society to which he belongs is the loser. A community that prefers its more easily assimilated writers cuts itself off from one of the main sources of the vitality that preserves it from the constant encroachment of materialism and banality.

It is only those few writers capable of imagining alternative societies who can enter into a serious and mutually advantageous relationship with their own. But, being deeply critical of it, their society fears to enter into a dialogue with them, which is what serious reading involves. Instead, they take to the writers who cause hardly a ripple in the deeper recesses of their minds, and thus these receive the public acclaim. They quickly become integrated into their society and serve a civic function in the same way as do lawyers, doctors or civil servants. If one were pressed to explain their precise task, they might be said to preserve communal cultural standards and present the national identity. They are in fact performing much the same function to their society as are the members of the Writers Union to Soviet Russia, though, admittedly, without being under the same pressures to do so.

As in several other western societies, the main body of our literature plays much the same part as it does in countries such as Russia and China. It is institutional and a function of state, while it is left to a very few dissidents (at certain times and in certain communities there are none at all) to preserve the true purpose of art as an instrument for the discovery of alternative concepts and new insights.

With us soon after the appearance of 'Ulysses' and a decade or so after our independence, there emerged a group of mainstream fiction writers, naturalistic, descriptive rather than probing, preoccupied with local colour and with an inherent conservatism. They were welcomed into the new political and social scene; they posed no awkward questions, imagined no alternatives, deferred gracefully to the world they and their readers had inherited. They were professional, witty, easy on tired or lazy minds, never obsessional or demanding. Their brushes with authority, as in the case of censorship, far from being any fundamental confrontation, were in the nature of family quarrels, for they shared almost all the religious, national and social assumptions of the community.

Indeed, in the thirties, looking back, there does not seem to have been a breath of effective dissent. Yeats, together with Shaw, inaugurated the Irish Academy of Letters to combat the censoring of serious books. But, partly because the aim was a too narrow one, the Academy did not achieve it, or indeed anything else of much significance, and soon became another small institution defending establishment art and subscribing to whatever is the literary equivalent of the political tenet of not rocking the boat.

The misconception of the function of imaginative writing persists. As long as it works as a pleasant semi-intellectual pursuit for readers and writers alike, no reason is seen in a community already sufficiently disrupted and disturbed, for not preserving the fairly comfortable literary status quo, its prizes and ideals.

This falsification of standards is achieved and preserved by the simple procedure of narrowing the literary horizon. Judgment is confined to a parochial milieu, and the tone-setters never make any comparisons with the highest contemporary achievements in other countries.

All is confined in a closed cultural circle, just as in Soviet Russia where members of the Writers Union create their own complacencies and self-satisfactions, protecting themselves from what is happening outside.

This mainstream literature, wherever operative, is closely woven into the general texture of the communal mind. It deals in types or characters that are easily recognisable, rather than in unique individuals, presents situations and relationships already familiar, while giving them a whimsical, pathetic or comical twist. Once this kind of writing has cut a channel through a society, it is difficult to set up a counter-current. The few genuine artists who remain outside the literary consensus make little impact inside their community which, in the belief that it already has a native literature that it can be proud of, a decorative and pleasing adjunct to its main preoccupations, rejects what disturbs, questions, offends, angers or may even be culturally and morally subversive. These writers will first be recognised and accepted outside their communities, as were Joyce, Beckett and, to some extent, Flann O'Brien, and later be let in by their own society through, so to speak, the back door.

While pieces of soft-centred fiction like Frank O'Connor's 'Guests of the Nation' and 'First Confession' were confirming an Irish public in its new mood of complacency and satisfaction at having, as well as its own brand of government and Church, an equally national and cosy literature, the obsessive and uncompromising art of Mr. Beckett was ignored. Here are the opening sentences of 'First Confession':

'All the trouble began when my grandfather died, and my grandmother – my father's mother – came to live with us. Relations in the one house are a trial at the best of times, but, to make it worse, my grandmother was a real old countrywoman, and quite unsuited to the life in town. She had a fat, wrinkled old face, and, to my mother's indignation, went round the house in bare feet–the boots had her crippled, she said.'

This writing–knitting would be a better word–is to the expected pattern or formula, the one then in fashion, and indeed by no means discarded today. Familiar sayings and attitudes are echoed with a nudge of humorous intent, the curtains are drawn, the fire poked, and a nice little tale with a whimsical slant is about to be told. No passion, no interior obsession, no real or outrageous comedy as in Flann O'Brien, Joyce or Mr. Beckett. In contrast, here is a passage from the latter's 'Molloy.' It is Moran's account of a conversation with his parish priest:

'He informed me that Mrs. Clement, the chemist's wife and herself a highly qualified chemist, had fallen, in her laboratory, from the top of a ladder, and broken the neck–. The neck! I cried. Of her femur, he said, can't you let me finish. He added that it was bound to happen. And I, not to be outdone, told him how worried I was about my hens, particularly my grey hen, which would neither brood or lay and for the past month and more had done nothing but sit with her arse in the dust, from morning till night. Like Job, haha, he said. I too said haha. What a joy it is to laugh, from time to time, he said... A brief silence ensued. What do you feed her

on, he said. Corn chiefly, I said. Cooked or raw? he said.
Both, I said. I added that she ate nothing anymore. Nothing!
he cried. Next to nothing, I said. Animals never laugh, he
said. It takes us to find that funny, I said loudly. He mused.
Christ never laughed either, he said, so far as we know... He
looked at me. Can you wonder? I said. There it is, he said. He
smiled sadly. She has not the pip, I hope, he said. I said she
had not, certainly not, anything he liked, but not the pip.'

This of course, is not naturalistic description. The mass of
detail at the start has a different tone from the plodding,
serious details of relationship in the O'Connor piece. It
evokes the desultory, inconsequent kind of conversation that
is universal and it doubtless causes discomfort rather than
cosy reassurance in the reader who needs to feel on familiar
ground.

It is imaginative writing of a kind not reached by the
O'Connor group, and had it been, as part of the mainstream
literature, assimilated by the reading community, it would
have widened, instead of narrowing, the thought-patterns of
our society.

Things may be even worse in England where since Lawrence,
if one excepts Evelyn Waugh, there has been no noticeable
counter-current to the main, shoddy stream, tributaries of
which are hailed every Sunday in the literary supplements. As
against this, intelligent English people seem more aware than
we are that the decline, however gentle, in a community, cannot be reversed by economic or social means alone. National
energy, the will, not just to survive but to excel, can only be
restored psychically, which is to say within the imagination.

In the past societies achieved this through their myth-
ologies or religions. Today, it is by exposing the minds of religious orders to the shock of original writing that a community ensures its organic growth.

Photo by Liam F. Miller

Juanita Casey was born in 1925 and comes from gypsy stock on both sides of her family. 'Restless and independent,' as she says herself, neither a conventional education nor a conventional life suited her. Largely self-taught, her literary technique depends on personal experience and sensibility. She was first married at sixteen, and has lived a nomadic life ever since. She derives much of her inspiration from her familiarity, since childhood, with animals and with travelling people. She has published two novels, a volume of poems, and a book of short stories.

JUANITA CASEY

Hemisphere

1971

O MR. FUGIT. Please, Mr. Fugit. Please don't hit the walnut tree. Said the little girl. You'll hurt the Holy Ghost. He feels it terribly, all through him, when you hit the tree. A woman, a spaniel, and a walnut tree, the more you beat'em the better they be, sang Mr. Fugit, hissing through his three black teeth. When he was busy, or thinking, or doing both together with a grimy frown, Mr. Fugit's tongue pressed against the black teeth like the overlapping pink bulges of a sow asleep against a tarred fence, and when he sang or shouted or became excited, the words frothed and sprayed out through them like a choppy sea against the remaining posts of a ruined break-water. Mr. Fugit was excited by many things. By a blunt scythe, a wrong-sized flower pot, the wind under his hat, slugs, bullfinches, mating dogs, Filthy buggers at it again, Garn you filthy buggers and a wildly flung hee, Budgets, un-expected kittens, the vagaries of a succession of totally deranged employers, small boys on sight, omens in the sky, late cuckoos, Saint Martin's Little Summer and hornets. Mr. Elijah Fugit was also hoping shortly to leave behind what he called his Mortal Coil. The little girl used to watch him wind up the long, ribbed, heavy hose, and wait expectantly for the chariot and horses of fire which Mr. Fugit apparently ex-pected to scorch down into the orchard and rocket him away to his Better Home Up There. Like me namesake, said Mr. Fugit, Like thic other wold Elijah in the Book. One Day. You'll see. One Day. The little girl, fascinated, would follow the dribbling end of the hose as it gobbled and gargled and helplessly obeyed Mr. Fugit's sea-faring hand over hand at the end of each afternoon, until Mr. Fugit had wound up the whole of the mortal coil onto its heavy iron frame, still vacantly dripping from its lolling end, and then Mr. Fugit would grind slowly off down the drive with a plume of kale bowing from the back of his knapsack. Slowly, squarely, with a spit on the road as he clipped the gate, and the silence returning up the disappointed gravel like an old spaniel on a hot day.

When Mr. Fugit had gone, the Holy Ghost would come out of the walnut tree in the orchard. He preferred the weekends, naturally, when Mr. Fugit wasn't there, but late afternoons were very pleasant, and so was the occasional morning when Mr. Fugit was employed elsewhere in the garden. But not too early. It was chilly then, and much too clear, and the grass tiresomely damp for sitting on. The Holy Ghost detested rain. He tried very hard never to get caught out in it, and therefore he seldom appeared to the little girl until well into May. But as he became so engrossed in his book that he sometimes sat on nettles, and had to be gently reminded and moved by the little girl, it was unfortunate that he did occasionally get absentmindedly drenched during a thunderstorm, and then he would have to dry his wings thoroughly, steaming and fluffing in the sun before returning into the walnut tree for the night. The Holy Ghost's wings were of beautifully overlapping laurel leaves, and the clatter and swish he made drying them worried the little girl, who was afraid Mr. Fugit would hear and come to investigate, bearing down on them and breathing hard like a righteous mastiff.

The Holy Ghost had first arrived because the little girl had thought he was there, and there he was. Sitting in the nettles, rather early in April, after a sharp shower. Drops of rain still fell from the leaves of his wings, and glittered in the bright sunlight. His big, flat, pale green feet in their wet sandals were hidden in the long grass, and he was reading in his green book, absorbed. I'm Drusilla, said the little girl. I'm the Holy Ghost, dear child, said the Holy Ghost, looking up with a pale green smile. You can't sit in those nettles, said the little girl. I didn't mean you to sit in the nettles. O, I hadn't really noticed, dear child, said the Holy Ghost, sitting down again in a sunnier corner, without rising. I'm sorry about the long grass, it needs cutting! Said the little girl, apologetically. Mr. Fugit will cut it tomorrow, beginning at eight-thirty a.m. and ceasing without visible reluctance at four-fortyfive p.m., said the Holy Ghost. He will then have finished it, except for around the apple trees, the Morello cherry, and that corner over there by the incinerator where at four-twentythree p.m. he is due to discover a grass snake's eggs. And as he will harbour neither viper in his bosom nor unspecified snake in the grass, I am quoting Mr. Fugit of course, he will employ the remainder of his time consigning them to hell and the incinerator. O, I've never seen a snake's eggs, said the little girl. What are they like? Hemispherical said the Holy Ghost. Indeed, we are all hemispherical, Drusilla. As you can already see, dear child, we inhabit the hemispheres of ourselves and the world. Half in one world, half in the next. I *love* Hemisphere! said the Holy Ghost rapturously, clasping his hands. It is a nice word, said the little girl, agreeably. Hemisphere, Hemisphere, warbled the Holy Ghost. Where have you been? Said the little girl. No, no, no, no, no, said the Holy Ghost, opening his eyes like a horrified turbot. No. Just Hemisphere. That's all. The little girl thought about it. Yes. You could wear hemisphere on your finger, a lovely blue ring, or you could buckle it all around the world with a clasp of stars, or you could hold it in a green bottle up to the light and wash your mauve hair with it, or you could whisper it to a mirror, who would breathe it back, or you could run with it like a hedgehog with a dry leaf stuck on a prickle, or you could watch it come out of a fish's mouth and ring across the pond like musical silence. You could see it balanced just in the middle of a cow's horns, spinning on the nose of a seal, in one whole day of a whale, bubbling in the world's retort of sea and sky, and in the tiniest thought that would one day be a flea in a flea's egg. After that, silence. But still hemisphere. Still there was hemisphere. Hemisphere, she said. Dear child, but of course, said the Holy Ghost. Isn't that just what I've been saying. And he sighed with a flock of pigeons overhead. Where will you go, said the little girl, supposing someone should come into the orchard? The walnut tree, said the Holy Ghost. I shall go into the walnut tree. And he did, just to show her. And that is how the Holy Ghost lived in the walnut tree, in Mr. Fugit's orchard, with his laurel leaf wings, his green book and his green smile, but frowning a foggy black Hemisphere when Mr. Fugit hit the tree on passing, which donged him all over and loosened a leaf or two. But when it rained the sort of rain that made utterly wet hens in slimy runs, the Holy Ghost, literally bored stiff in the walnut tree, knitted himself a long green Testament, and wound it around his neck, as he said it Came In Useful On A Rainy Day. Then, when the sun came out, the Holy Ghost would sit all over the orchard, wherever he and the little girl thought or didn't think, and birds flew through him, and a grasshopper sat on the corn on his little toe, reading his book and saying a wide golden Hemisphere, while a nuthatch examined his knothole ear for a nesting site. And all the while he read his green book, and smiled his green smile, and nothing was written on the book at all. Which, the Holy Ghost said, when questioned by the little girl, was because it was the Last Word. And being the Last, dear child, there is no need of it, as no one has ever seen it. And the Holy Ghost smiled a calm blue Hemisphere.

When the September mists came again, the Holy Ghost

decided that the now heavily falling apples were a gross impediment to his reading, that frosted sandals, an insipient chilblain on his corn and a chilly wind up the tree trunk, were not conducive to another winter in a British orchard, and besides he was really needed all over all the Hemispheres, willy nilly. Willy Nilly, said the Holy Ghost to the little girl, on his last morning in her company, Dear child. She tried to think him back, but he was shrinking with the last shreds of mist on the river. Promise me one thing. He was almost gone now. Promise me one thing, dear child. I go around and around and around the Wicked World, and I read my book, and I sit under the trees in the orchard, and everywhere I go I try to find someone, just someone, who will spare a drop of water for the gudgeon in the carriage rut. The walnuts had all been picked, the leaves were black and curling on the walnut tree. I promise, Willy Nilly, said the little girl, and the Holy Ghost murmuring a fond, pale Hemisphere, wove gently through the smoke of Mr. Fugit's dying bonfire, and by the time the wood pigeon had clapped his wings, vanished. The little girl went up for tea, and Mr. Elijah Fugit came down to dampen the now thoughtful bonfire for the night. Mr. Fugit trudged down the path and kicked through a pile of freshly dropped laurel leaves. Bleedin' kid, said Mr. Fugit. Untidy little buggers. And picked up an old stretched sandal from the long grass around the dormant bonfire. Must take a size eighteen, remarked Mr. Fugit, as he threw it onto the ashes. Don't know no-one round these parrrts with bleedin' great feet like thaat. Big as a bleedin' lily pond. And at that very moment, in the village of Hung-Lung, in the province of Chang-yi, a little boy poured a can of water into a dry cart rut. On his way back he would rescue the little fish lying in it, and return it to the river. And he wondered as he did so, who had said Hemisphere so warmly in rainbow Chinese, when there was no one in the road but himself and one small gudgeon.

JUANITA CASEY

The Well

1972

THE OLD man was scything the lane's verges outside the chained gate into the fields of the old house. Swatches of knapweed and long grass, peppered with heads of yarrow, froze as though shocked by the sliding scythe, and fell in smooth sheets, the occasional defiant nettle or stalk of meadowsweet refusing to capitulate entirely, and sticking out of the scented waves like the boy's stubborn back whisker. The boy's hair was the colour of old thatch, ruffled and spiky as a cold bird's feathers. Not supposed to go up there, young un. No one there now, anyway. The boy kicked a stone. The old man blew his nose, and settled the dark blue handkerchief back into his pocket. From the back of his belt he pulled out a wetstone, and shouldered the scythe's sweeping blade. I doubt if they'll find a buyer in a hurry, neither. T'es too big, lad. Awkward old place. Though there be good land there. Ar, good land right enough. The long blade rang in the heat as he sharpened it with easy sweeps. A few short, sharp strokes on the curved end, and he looked round for the boy. The boy had gone. All young varmints. Every durned one of them, said the old man, scratching the back of his walrus neck. He looked up at the arched bower of elms over his head. A silent rook stared down through the branches. The elm leaves hung flat in the heat. In the valley a white poplar glittered as a spiral of wind shimmered around it. With a patter like heavy rain approaching, a flock of sheep rustled into the shade of the hedge behind the old man. They stood panting, heads down, ears listless, the occasional explosive cough loud as a squib.

One by one they knelt and lay down on the dusty earth beneath the high elms, and the sound of their cudding and the interthreading of bees clicked like a loom weaving the humming afternoon. Thunder soon, said the old man, sniffing like a dog. The rook planed down into the sunlight, stroked four lazy, rowing wingbeats over the valley, and soared up into another stand of elm trees a mile away.

The boy ran through the long grass around the edge of the field. He didn't want to be seen from the village. To his left, a long avenue of elms ran parallel with the field, ending by the farm buildings. The boy knew a long drive lay beneath their shade, passing the barns and the cowsheds, the tractor and implement sheds, and the stables. The big house stood at the end of the drive, within a high-walled garden. There were steps, and ornamental iron gates, a flagstone path across a lawn, and a great broken cedar, with one branch leaning like an elbow on the lawn. More ornamental iron gates led to other parts of the old house's gardens, from the front lawns into the vegetable garden, and from the vegetable garden into a small, walled orchard. Around the back, the same high, stone walls enclosed a grass plot with a big pink-flowered chestnut tree, and a broken well-head with no rope left on its bare roller, a solidly rusted handle, and only level grass across the hole where the well had once been. A rusty bucket with no bottom lay beside it. The boy had reached the chestnut tree. He leaned against the wall, and with his mouth open, strained back and gagged up into its layers of green leaves, trying to see the blue sky through them. But the leaves were as dense as a jungle, secret and folded upon each other like long green hands. The boy felt as though he was beneath the roof of a cool, green cathedral. He ran out into the hot sunlight again, and looked up at the great tree, with its tiers of pink candle-flowers, its lower branches deeply curtsying to the ground, and within them the dark tent of shade he had just left. The boy went over to the well. He toed at the bucket, and jumped as it fell over with a rattle. He looked guiltily over to the silent house. Red rust powdered the toe of his shoe. A small, ornamental gate led into a smaller stone courtyard, and the back windows and back door of the house. The boy looked up at its roof undulating against the sky in great curves and sweeps like the back and shoulders of a sleeping stone beast. The small tiles lay one upon the other like the thick leaves of an old book, and the boy remembered the white fantails which used to strut and dip and slide on the roof when people lived here. Before they went away. Dry chalky splashes still flecked the courtyard. The boy wondered who else would come to the old house, and would they keep white fantails too. It would be nice to see cattle again in the unkept fields, not the homely old mixed Shorthorns though, his father had said. The new people would probably go in for a checker-board of Friesians, and no horses anywhere. The boy had never been up to the old house before, and had always wanted to see it. From the village you could see the cloud of white fantails blowing over the roofs and settling on them like a thrown handful of May blossom.

The boy looked into the lower windows. A long, black kitchen range, a sink, an old calendar. A green wall, that must be the kitchen. It was too dark to see anything else. The back door was shabby for such a big house, he thought. Very ordinary. The panels were gnawed and frayed in one place, where kicking boots had ratted the years out of it, and the wood around the handle by the big lock was bare and greasy, and the dull grey paint blistered and worn. The other room was bright with bare, uncurtained sunlight, the leaded front windows patterning the floor like a bright strip from a gir-affe's neck, thought the boy. A white door was open into the sunny room, but the boy couldn't see round it. A stone-roofed shed held a pile of logs, a smell of mice and mould and old hens, some stiff, grey harness with rusty rings and cobwebbed chains, a bicycle frame, a green boot, and a parasol of black fungi in a corner. The boy examined everything but nothing was worth the squiggle inside of illicit appropriation. The north wall of the house was like a fortress, only two small windows very high up. The boy went round the side of the house, climbed over another, lower wall, and peered through the decorative gates at the front. The lawn was like a hayfield, and its great hanging branch gave the gigantic cedar the appearance of a dismasted barque caught on a lapping grass reef. The front windows of the house stared out at the boy, straight browed beneath their stone mullions, their frowning emptiness like the gaze of a blind man listening. The front door was of heavy, panelled wood, with church hinges. The boy knew exactly the sound it made, closing. He didn't know why. He just did. He pushed the gates aside, and closed them again after him. They had no catch, which surprised him. He was a long time climbing about on the cedar, bouncing on the long, springing fingers sweeping the grass like a raven's wing. Tiring, the boy jumped to the ground. He leaned against the cedar's rough trunk, and looked up through the ordered and majestic branches, the reeling blue spaces between them a kaleidoscope of light and silence. The great goat-horned top spire was motionless in the sky above him, as though the thing that was really the tree had withdrawn aloofly and was living at the very top, looking down on everyone below with the long, circling stare of an owl. The boy picked up one of its fallen cones, and pressed its stiff, open scales against his nose, inhaling the dry, faint smell. Old books, thought the boy. Old wooden chests. He wandered through the warm, long grass towards the other iron gate. Someone had left a pile of blue material in a corner of the high wall, like an old, blue-green silk dress. He went closer. A strong smell lifted from the corner. Something's died, thought the boy. Phew. He saw first the metallic blue body of a fly detach itself from the other blue-green mass, and circle tightly before buzzing down again onto it. Then he saw that it was a dead peacock crouched against the wall, its long, lustrous neck bent backwards towards one fanned wing, the eye an empty black socket through which the fly reappeared as he watched, to tilt and run back again. Somewhere inside the bird's head, he heard its muffled buzzing. The boy saw the dry, scaled black legs with their claws clutched together, and the ordinary looking chestnut wing feathers among the iridescence and shine of the rest of its body. Like any old hen's, thought the boy. The glorious tail lay in a tangled sheaf, golden-brown and curiously hidden and camouflaged in the surrounding grass. Only when the boy moved, the iridescence sprang and shivered down the shafts of each long feather, its tremulous fringes of mingled blue and gold trembling like antennae, the compelling, changing green eyes at the ends swelling in perfect scale, from the smaller side feathers to the great, cobra-headed stare of the fan's centre. The boy pulled one away from the body. The quill stank, with pieces of rotten flesh adhering to it, and the boy dropped it again. He would never be allowed to bring it into the house, back home. The little black-pinned crown feathers were still there, like sensitive green keys for tuning the whole instrument that had been the living, vibrating bird. The boy remembered how you could hear the yelps of the peacocks over in the village on a westerly wind. Rain's coming, everyone would say. Listen to the peacocks, rain's coming. He wondered whether the people had taken the others with them, and why this one had been left. Why had it died, angled into this corner, and left to disintegrate like the pile of feathers from a plucked Sunday cockerel. The boy longed for some eye feathers, but the stench sickened him. He smelled his fingers, relieved to find that they weren't tainted. He pushed open the ornamental gate, and went through into a high-walled jungle of grass and weeds, which had once been a kitchen garden. Ragged, knee-high box hedges edged the gravel paths, the stones nearly hidden beneath the encroaching crowns of dandelions and pressing daisies. It was very hot, and the boy picked a stray bunch of pastel columbines, then threw them away, high into the air. They arched and fell like a flight of shot, bright, long-tailed birds into the long grass. It was too hot inside the high walls, and the boy saw that through the next iron gate there was an orchard with a tangle of apple trees in it. It would be nice to sit down in the shade of an apple tree, he thought. He had to push the gate hard, lifting and grunting to get it open far enough for him to squeeze through. It was a very small orchard, he realised, and there were only a few very big and old, gnarled and lichened apple trees in it. He saw that the high walls were broken and crumbling in one place, and that there was an old wooden door at the far end. And he saw that here the grass was not long. It had been grazed, bitten down nearly bare. At the same time he saw piles of droppings beneath one wall, and smelled a hot, leonine, curiously strong smell. A horse, thought the boy, excited, and looking around as he went forward. Waves of heat beat against the walls soundlessly. The boy was stifled and breathless, the hot smell of the invisible horse pulsating on the walls. He walked slowly from one apple tree to another, and then noticed there was a small thicket of brambles and elder bushes around an old fallen walnut at the far corner. He could see two black ears flicking, and a head nodding quickly up and down in the shade. The boy wished he had an apple, or that he could pick a handful of long grass to offer the hidden horse. Hello, horse, said the boy, shading his eyes as he approached the thicket from the front. The uprooted tree in the rough corner enclosed a tunnel of shade, and he saw what he thought were lines of sunlight and shadow striping the horse as it moved out towards him. Like the way a pike glides through the weeds, and you can't tell which are the green and silver stripes of fish or water or weed, thought the boy. But the stripes didn't flicker and draw back to fall and dapple the ground behind it, as the animal stepped into the sunlight. The boy saw the long head with its dazzle of puzzled striping like a maze down the forehead, the round, magpie ears turned on to him like funnels, the black, polished eyes whetted to a shining malice, the whole of the incredible, flashing body with its painted strokes of intense black and white, the ripple of the rounded trot as it quickened towards him, and the small, dangerous hooves which the zebra placed lightly and precisely with a weaving motion like a snake. The boy, even as he ran, thought the zebra not so much an animal as a striking snake. He backed behind a tree. The zebra had lost sight of him. It stopped, whisked its tail's brush with whipping strokes against its flanks, and shook the high frill of its mane which rippled like a black and white fin. It lifted its tail, and dropped some hard balls of dung. Then it looked round with an intent black glitter, the sun sparkling in one eye, and stretching out its head, barked angrily like a dog. The flaring bands on its body shook and rippled. The boy saw that it was much quicker than a horse, that it had an intensity, a feline, white-hot fire behind the bars of its painted hide. Its restless padding held the nervousness of tigers, the black, unstable stare unfathomable as jet. The zebra began to walk tightly, very close to the walls, its muzzle to the ground, snuffing out spurts of dust in long, rooting snorts. Its mane shook and fluttered with each quick step. The boy knew it was looking for him. He stared round at the walls. He knew he could never reach the iron gate before the zebra chopped him, drilling him into the hot, bare ground with its spiralled forelegs. There was only one place in the wall which he could just reach, with a pile of fallen stones from which to jump up. He wasn't even thinking now. Nervously and deliberately, the zebra paced along the wall to the iron gate. It stopped, laid back its long ears, and barked through it. A cuckoo hurtled over the wall with a loud, bubbling laugh, and wheeled up into the top of the cedar, the male bird following and calling. Fluttering and balancing with their long tails, they mated, and the female flew off again, silently. The male bird remained in the tree, wavering and flapping, then planed down and flew after his mate. The boy heard him call again over the valley. The zebra had shied as the birds' flight rushed overhead, bunching its body and hurling it sideways like a striped ball. It trotted into a corner. Then it froze, glaring. The boy realised that the zebra could now see him by the tree and sped like a whippet for the wall. He heard the tattoo of hooves behind him, and heard the dull double snap of the zebra's teeth as he jumped. He scrambled up onto the broken part of the wall, and looked down, shivering. The zebra had stumbled on the fallen stones, unable to get near enough to bite up at him. It trotted, whisking, to the shade of the nearest tree, and wheeled round beneath it, its long ears nervously flicking. The boy saw that the wall on the other side was too high to jump from. The level of the orchard was much higher here, and the walls were nearly twenty feet above a narrow lane to the fields beyond. The boy eased himself on the hard wall, scattering a shower of crumbling powder and small stones. The zebra jumped, its ears pressed back against its neck, the high mane arched between them like a Grecian helmet. The heat breathed like an animal down the hedges, and the sun and the zebra seemed to the boy to be merging. He saw the sun caged in the dazzling orchard, and the yellow teeth of the zebra grinding overhead. Now the boy thought of circuses, of how the zebra had got in, of the shut door and the closed gate, of zoos, of the new people. And how to get down. Please God get me down. *O God, Please.* He wasn't imagining it. It was a zebra. A zebra. He said aloud, A zebra. A long growl of thunder muttered behind him. It was very silent now, still, waiting. No wind stirred, nothing scratched the mind into listening within the bowl of silence. He felt congealed, as though caught inside one facet of a compound eye, like a fly crawling soundlessly in the amber silence. The zebra stood glassily motionless in the ringing heat. Another black tongue of thunder licked at the boy. Behind him, down in the fields, the trees blazed with unnatural, incandescent heads against the indigo sky, a last flame of defiance before they were extinguished beneath the dark, shouldering weight of the approaching storm. A bright fizz of lightning spat silently behind the trees. The boy waited for the thunder's rolling growl, which was now much nearer. A sneaking wind lifted the wet hair at the back of his neck. The stones were hurting his bare knees, and he was as cramped and stiff now as a pinned insect. A faint humming sound stirred the air, so faint it was like the ghost of a sound. Somewhere above the old house. He was uneasy. What was it, what was coming. He strained and listened. It was like a swarm of bees coming. The boy clung to the wall as above the roof a great balloon floated serenely, the wind humming among its ropes, and the basket carried along beneath it like a square dot under a big, swinging exclamation mark, thought the boy. He didn't dare look up or crane too hard, in case he lost his balance. With the inexorable, unfolding growth of a dream, the balloon passed overhead, and the faint humming died away. It was white, with broad red stripes and it silently drifted away over the fields. The zebra still stood silently beneath the apple tree. In silence the boy watched the balloon starkly and lividly illuminated against the black wall of sky building up against it, and then, still in terrible silence, suddenly, the round striped ball was ringed by a crown of orange flames, which licked up the sides in leaping tongues, and engulfed the whole balloon in a blazing ball of fire. Then a white fragment like a falling handkerchief, and it spiralled down trailing a bright orange plume of flame behind it. It dropped behind the hills, and a long black, feather of rising smoke etched a thin line on the dark and empty sky. Even as the boy watched, it melted and vanished. A wall of rain spears blotted the hills, and the fierce light on the heads of the trees died away. As he clung to the wall, shivering and sobbing, the boy could hear his heart thumping like a rabbit's, and in the silence, with the black now nearly overhead, he heard the sound of someone winding the squeaking handle of a well. In the small grass yard, where the startling pink flowers on the great chestnut tree were alight like massed candles against the coming storm.

Photo by Roy Alexander

Michael Foley was born in Derry, Northern Ireland, in 1947, and was educated there and at Queens University, Belfast, where he took a degree in chemistry and did research in computer science. His poetry has appeared in magazines and book form– a first collection, 'True Life Love Stories' was published in 1976 (Blackstaff Press). He wrote a satirical column for several years in 'Fortnight,' a political review, and is the author of many short stories. He is a former co-editor of 'The Honest Ulsterman.' Married, he now lives in London, working as a teacher.

MICHAEL FOLEY

The Joy Beyond All Telling

1976

I

ALTHOUGH IT is several generations since my family have lived
in the west of Ireland I have maintained an odd connection
with that part of the world. Every Friday afternoon I brave the
bombs and bullets of this malevolent Northern city and make
for a small newsagent's shop where I collect my regular order
– *The Western Tribune, The Connaught People,* and *The Munster
Democrat.* No doubt it will be assumed that I do this in a
spirit of satire and contempt – but it is not so. It is more an
urge to experience an innocent world, although innocence is
perhaps not the right word; let us say a world of total belief, a
world with that sense of timelessness that is at once so
valuable and rare, occurring only in a few charmed works of
art – *Alice in Wonderland, The Pickwick Papers,* the detective
stories of Raymond Chandler.

So it was that on a miserable Friday in late September I
passed through the wire mesh that encloses the city centre,
subjected myself to the indignity of the 'frisk' and sought out
the side street that harboured P. J. Brennan's paper shop. At
this point I had been collecting my order for almost two years
and, after months of conjecture, Mr Brennan had come to the
conclusion that I was some sort of Gaelic sports freak. Every
visit was graced with sporting anecdotes, such as now as he
told me of Ballina's victory in a hurley match.

'They won it,' he told me without enthusiasm, 'but it's not
the same these days. I mind big Patsy Fahy going down the

pitch and – I saw this with my own eyes – I saw him open three men from there to there.' And his finger went down his face in a swift dramatic slash.

Outside black storm clouds had gathered in the sky, enhancing that sense of foreboding that hangs above the city at all times. Like the other passers-by I huddled tighter into my clothes and made for home, where I laid my precious burden on the floor and, after a moment of exquisite indecision, picked up *The Western Tribune*. At once a headline caught my eye:

Itinerant Acted Like Animal

On driving past his bog Mr Benny Dillon saw some tinker children with a bag. On driving past the tinkers' camp he said to Owen Ward, the defendant's father-in-law, he was surprised at him taking his turf. Then Paddy Ward, who had some drink taken, 'Went like an animal'. He pulled open the driver's door of the car and started kicking witness with his foot. He was 'firing' fists into car as hard as he could.

To Mr Oliver O'Donaghue, solr., defending, witness replied: 'Only for Owen Ward someone would have been killed in the car.'

Mrs Mary Dillon, wife of the complainant, said defendant used kicks and his fists and even went to hit the child in the back.

'I thought we were all killed,' she said. 'It was only the hand of God that saved us.'

Mr O'Donoghue: 'It was a first-class miracle that no one was marked.'

I paused, sighing deeply with pleasure. Outside the storm had broken and the rain was coming down like rods of steel, hissing furiously off the pavements as it fell. I picked up *The Connaught People* and glanced idly through the inner pages until I came on a small paragraph that made me sit up rigid with shock. It looked innocuous enough.

The Very Rev. Fr. Malachy Kilbane (P.P.) today officiated at the first 'folk-style' Mass in Spittoon. The music was provided by a group from Spittoon Boys'

Club, playing a variety of guitars and tambourines.

Knowing a little of Spittoon and Fr. Kilbane this item
seemed to me the most profound and shocking mystery I had
ever encountered. For Father Malachy Kilbane was the most
staunchly traditional of priests and it was unthinkable that he
could be involved in any kind of 'folk' Mass. I vividly recalled
him mounting the pulpit to face his congregation.

'I've been accused of scolding,' he'd begin, 'and I've been
accused of shouting.' Here he would pause and stare all
round the church, a look of defiance growing on his face.
Then he would grip the pulpit fiercely and scream with all his
power, 'BUT I'LL SHOUT...AND I'LL SCOLD...' going on
to denounce whatever failings had incurred his wrath that
week.

Throwing all my commitments to the winds I caught the
next bus to the West of Ireland.

II

Spittoon is a little village on the western seaboard, surrounded on three sides by the rocky townland of Drung and
on the fourth by the bleak and stormy Atlantic, from which
the dark rain clouds roll to be repulsed by the rocky hills and
release their contents on the tiny village. It is very often wet in
Spittoon.

However, when I arrived the following day the weather was
brilliant, uncannily so for that time of year. Whereas, in the
city I had left, the bitterness of a long winter was in the air,
here the sun shone with full midsummer power and there was
not the slightest trace of encroaching autumn. As our bus
came round the last bend of Drung Head the village of Spittoon below was a striking sight. The little crescent of
buildings sparkled in the sun, the fishing boats lay at rest in
the harbour and out at sea wild streaks of purple underlaid

the turquoise brilliance, producing an orgy of colour beyond the reach of even the most *farouche* of the abstract expressionists.

As we commenced the winding descent the jolts awoke an old countryman asleep on the front seat and, realising he had passed his stop, he sprang up with a wild grimace.

'Let me out,' he screamed, 'or Ah'll tummle the bus.' And he ran at the grinning driver clutching a parcel to his breast.

I took this opportunity to get out and walk, savouring the view on my half-hour descent to the village, where I registered at the Seaview Hotel. When the arrangements were complete I set out at once for the Parochial House.

I remembered Father Kilbane as a man with a forbidding countenance, a forceful impatient stride, a look of the most piercing shrewdness and a grip like that of a vice. The man I saw walking on the lawn was undoubtedly Father Kilbane – but his appearance had changed in some strange way. His once vicelike grip was now mild and limp and the keen eyes were vague and unfocused as though looking in upon himself. Nevertheless I proceeded with my plan, cocking my head and regarding him with a merry twinkle.

'Now, Father,' said I. 'I'd like you to renew your acquaintance with an old friend...an old friend by the name of *John Power*!' And so saying I produced the wrapped bottle with a flourish – but his response was uncomprehending and vague.

'John Power...? John Power...?' My little joke, a joy surely to the priest I had known, now seemed to have fallen flat. He looked from the bottle to my face in total amazement. 'No, Father. It's just... I wanted to find out... *about these folk masses*.'

'Ah no, son, no, no, there's been nothing like that here, none of that class of thing at all.'

Yet even as he spoke the denial his eyes lit up with joy and he left with a look of sheer ecstasy on his face.

I decided to make some enquiries in the village and called

on my old friend Sean Glynn, the local pharmacist and a man of some weight in the community. Knowing his uncle had recently died I seized his hand in a firm, manly grip.

'Sorry for your trouble, Sean.' Sean replied with a silent nod and putting an arm about my shoulder led me into his home. The uncle had been dying for a long time but I judged that the shock had been no less severe.

'He went very quick at the end.' I said.

'Ah he did, he did.' Sean gave me a sudden look of respect. 'He went very quick at the end.'

After several moments of dignified silence I addressed him again in a low serious tone.

'What're ye drivin' now, Sean?' I asked.

'Hillman Hunter.'

'Is she sore on juice?'

'About thirty – thirty-five.'

I nodded profoundly and there came between us a rich wonderful silence such as only occurs between mature males in perfect accord. It seemed a good time to put my question.

'Sean, what's all this about Father Kilbane?' At once the accord disappeared and his honest face became clouded and troubled. I saw that I would learn nothing and left almost at once.

On the way out I called into the shop to see his wife Nora. She was a handsome, intelligent woman with an interest in culture, too good for such a small place I often thought. We had been close in the past and I thrilled to see her again as she bent at her work with her back to me. Then she turned and I experienced something close to terror – for instead of her usual ironic grin her face shone with a brilliant ineffable joy, the same as I had seen an hour before on the features of Father Kilbane.

III

The next day was fine in the same uncanny way. I break-
fasted early and set out to climb Drung Head, avoiding the
main road and keeping to small paths. Already the sun was
strong and when I stopped for a rest half-way up I was
breathing heavily. I lay down in the bracken and observed
the bay below, basking, it appeared, in the timelessness of
full midsummer. It was worlds apart from the troubled
North, and I even forgot why I had come, falling into a
light doze there.

The voices of two women passing on the track above woke
me up with a start. The voices were genteel and well-to-do –
but the words would have shocked the most wildly super-
stitious of peasant women...

'I believe a bright light came first.' said one. 'A bright light
filled the whole place so they could hardly see. Then they
heard the music and he appeared.'

'Apparently.'

I sat up quickly, rigid with attention – but suddenly the first
voice dropped to an angry, authoritative bass.

'Timothy! Come down from those rocks. You'll be cut to
ribbons if you fall. And don't expect me to be running after
you to the Infirmary. Hoho no. Don't expect me to be running to the Infirmary.'

I climbed on again towards the summit, moving strongly
and swiftly now, as though the extra height would clarify the
mystery. But still the jigsaw pieces would not fit. What was the
change in Father Kilbane and why had he told me a deliberate
lie? Why was Sean Glynn so troubled and reticent and what
had happened to his beautiful wife? And now, on this brilliant morning, why were two worldly women discussing
apparitions and mysterious lights? I sat on a flat rock looking
far out to sea, turning the matter over in my mind – and I was
highly annoyed when I saw a short stocky figure climbing my

way. There was no doubt that he was bent on conversation and indeed he came straight towards me, grinning happily.

'That's the weather now. Ah? Ah?' And he looked at me closely as though the question had been quite profound.

'It certainly is.'

'On holiday are ye?'

'In a way.'

'Like meself. Ye'd be from the North then?' I nodded silently and he took off his cap to scratch his head. 'Do ye know this, ye wouldn't know what to make of it up there now. Ah?'

If there was one thing I did not want to discuss it was the state of affairs in the North. I responded with a shrug and a weak laugh, and was preparing to move off when his next sentence pulled me up short.

'Listen,' he said, 'Do ye not think there's something queer about this place?' I experienced a thrill of expectation but managed to stay calm. 'Ill' tell ye a funny story,' he went on. 'A couple of weeks ago there was a couple of tinker children stealin' turf. Sent to do it, ye know. And doesn't the owner of the bog spot them and follow them to the camp in his car...'

I interrupted, smiling a little.

'...where a fracas ensued involving Patrick Ward and the occupants of the car?'

'Do ye know all about it then?'

'Not entirely.'

'Well, there was a terrible scene, Ward kicking and punching going mad trying to get into the car and your man's wife and children in the back seat. A terrible carry-on, the police called and a court-case and everything. But wait till you hear the best of it. A week ago didn't the two of them meet head-on in the main street. A Garda rushed to separate them, but didn't Benny Dillon say it's alright, ye can have as much turf as ye want. And better still, the tinker says no, no, and takes out his wallet and hands over ten pounds for the stolen turf and another twenty-five for damage to the car.'

'And this tinker,' I questioned urgently 'was there a strange look of joy on his face?'

'You're dead right. How did ye know? He had the rarest look Ah ever saw – as if he'd just won the Pools or something.'

IV

But the piecemeal nature of my discoveries is of little interest and it is time to tell the story of what happened in Spittoon.

It was a pleasant Sunday in August, and Father Kilbane was on his way to the church to say Mass, shooing the malingerers before him in his usual brusque way, He changed into his vestments in the sacristy and the Mass proceeded with nothing more untoward than a few scowls and grunts at the altar boys. At the end of the first Gospel he mounted the pulpit to begin his sermon but, as always, refused to start until everyone standing at the back had moved up. A few diehards swaggered out, but the majority slouched up the aisles in hang-dog fashion, and Father Kilbane began in clear, ringing tones.

'It is the smart thing today,' he said, 'to complain about pollution. We can hardly pick up a newspaper or switch on the T.V. without someone complaining about pollution – the pollution of the atmosphere, the pollution of rivers, the pollution of seas, etcetera, etcetera, etcetera.' He paused to let the truth of this sink in. 'But do we ever hear anyone complaining about the worst pollution of all, the pollution of souls – the pollution due to cinemas and T.V. screens, the pollution of a cinema in this very village *and the people eatin' it not to mind lookin' at it.*'

He was getting into full swing now and the congregation braced itself. It was then that the strange events began. The sunlight had been falling through the windows in isolated beams but now it seemed to gather strength and spread until a tremendous brilliance filled the church and the congregation could scarcely see, the pulpit especially beyond their vision, as though draped in a veil of gold. At the same time they experienced an inner change. They were purged as if they had passed through the fires of Purgatory and were entering Paradise, a world quickened and glorified and bounteous with pleasures. Their faces became illuminated, glowing with ineffable joy, and they saw, through the veil of gold, not Father Kilbane, but a handsome young priest who was smiling upon them with the utmost sweetness.

The subsequent descriptions were vague. Some said he had brown curly hair and a beard, others said he was cleanshaven with straight black hair. What everyone agreed on was his outlook. One woman described him as 'real with-it;' another as 'real mod.' Many claimed that he was a young priest from a neighbouring parish, one who had been fired for his progressive views, who had left the priesthood and married a nurse and been knocked down by a bus in Glasgow.

At any rate, this young man left the pulpit and came slowly among them down the centre aisle.

'You all know,' he said, 'how fairy lights work. If you have fairy lights on a Christmas tree and if one of these lights doesn't work, then none of them will work, and the tree won't light. I want you to be like those fairy lights. I want every one of you to get plugged in, and I want everyone of you to shine so the tree will light.'

He raised his arms and turned slowly round to face each section of the congregation in turn. The light shone more brightly again, the veil of gold reformed before their eyes and they heard an exquisite music, as though a band of joyful teenagers were singing some gay song, in the background a happy-go-lucky music of guitars and tambourines.

'There were such songs that my heart was full of joy,' said

one old man. 'There was a song like Heaven in the air,' said a woman, equally enthralled.

As the song and music swelled, the congregation with one accord joined hands, pioneers with drunken labourers, matrons with garage mechanics, itinerants with T. D.'s, teachers with easy women, Gardai with teddy-boys home from England, brother with feuding brother, and husband with warring wife. All knelt as one and the world was rectified and glowing and a penitent people beat upon their breasts and cried out in wonder and their tears were like rain of the mountains on their cheeks.

V

Was it all a hallucination? The phenomenon of collective hallucination is not unknown, a phantasmal image passed from person to person by a kind of telepathy. Was it some kind of mystical experience? A survivor of a bomb explosion in one of our Northern cities has described how, in the few seconds between the flash and the bang, he relived his entire adult life – and at the same pace as it first occured. Was it some strange effect of light? The discoveries of modern science have shown just how tenuous is our grasp on the real, and it has been estimated that there is a chance in fifty-five million of a brick rising four feet from the ground of its own accord.

What cannot be disputed are the effects of that Sunday morning. Some of these have already been described, for instance the conversion of Father Kilbane that first drew my attention to the whole affair. This was even more dramatic than I had imagined. Not only had he begun folk-style masses, but he had acquired a second-hand minibus and drove his youthful musicians round all the neighbouring parishes. Their enthusiasm was infectious, but it left little time for his usual pursuits and he allowed his membership of the Golf Club to expire, an event all the more surprising when one remembers that he had been strongly fancied for the Captain's Prize.

Then there was the painful case of Nora Glynn. I have already remarked that she was a cultured woman, and her ruling passion was the local Dramatic Society, in all of whose productions she had played leading roles. Her talent had won the praise of every Festival adjudicator in the land, but she had let herself down by her liaison with Eddie Mahon, the leading man. Awful things were predicted for the day when Sean found out. 'It's the quiet ones you want to watch,' they said – and 'Sean's a wild quiet fella but he's a terrible man when he starts.'

Yet on the Sunday of the strange appearance Nora Glynn confessed all to her husband. Eddie Mahon went with her, and far from killing each other, Sean and he became firm friends, attending the dogs in Kiltimagh every Thursday night.

Another strange about-turn was effected by Con O'Brien, proprietor of the Seaview Hotel and the local T. D. For many years he had led a vigorous campaign against itinerants, repeating that their camps were eyesores, an insult to any decent Irishman and a barrier to tourism and the efforts of those working for progress. Yet, under the spell of the mod priest, this same man threw open the doors of the Seaview Hotel, accepting an entire encampment for an indefinite period.

Perhaps strangest of all was the wedding of Seamie McIvor and Roisin Molloy. A date had been fixed for some time, but at the last minute the unfortunate groom was thrown out of work and the girl's father, a small hill-farmer, was unable to meet the expense. At one point it looked as though the ceremony would have to be postponed.

'And me with me going-away outfit bought and everything.' Thus wailed the unfortunate bride – but far from being put off, or even curtailed, this wedding became the focal point for all the joy and magnanimity of that strange time.

First a wedding dress arrived from Nora Glynn, a magnificent creation in organza and guipure lace; then a three-tiered cake with figurines, a present from the Shiels sisters, a formidable quartet of spinsters who also took over the catering. Seamie McIvor was not left out. Eddie Mahon drove up to his door and delivered crate upon crate of lager and stout. Father Kilbane sent a case of Johnnie Walker and took over the ceremony from the young curate originally booked. Many said his sermon was the finest ever heard in those parts.

'On the thirty-first of July nineteen and sixty-nine,' he began, 'the astronauts first stepped out onto the moon. That is a day that will go down in the history books and be talked about for all times. Yet just as important as that is the marriage of Seamus and Roisin here today.'

Con O'Brien opened the Seaview Hotel for the reception and somehow managed to book the internationally famous 'top-liners,' the Florida Showband (who, it must be remembered, were still riding high in the charts with *Please Mr. Psychiatrist*).The Shiels sisters pulled out every stop, demonstrating their famous motto, 'Put the few shillings to it and do the job right.' Food and drink were available in abundance and guests from every walk of life mingled as freely as they had on that memorable morning in the church.

With the Florida Showband as a competent backing group, the afternoon sparkled with traditional and contemporary music, song and dance. Eddie Mahon sang *The Story of a Starry Night* and Benny Dillon got an enthusiastic response for the well-loved ballad *In the Dock a Ship was Anchored on a Bright Saint Patrick's Day*. Sean Glynn sang a special request, *Our Heavenly Mother*, and after many entreaties and rounds of applause Father Malachy Kilbane was coaxed onto the stage and enthralled the audience with his rendering of *Cutting the Corn in Creeslough*.

After several hours the young couple left in Sean Glynn's Hillman Hunter, very kindly loaned them for touring in the

South – but their departure had little effect on events in the Seaview, where the celebrations continued far into the night.

VI

When I returned from Spittoon my affairs took some setting in order and it was several weeks before I was back in Brennan's. At once Mr. Brennan produced a vast pile of back issues which he dropped on the counter with a reproachful look.

'I've actually been down in the West,' I explained and he brightened up a little at this.

'Did ye see any hurley at all?'

'I'm afraid I didn't have time.'

'Ah mebbe it's just as well.' His head drooped in shame. 'Kiltimagh were hammered again.'

I took the papers and hurried home, anxious for news of Spittoon. But the news was scarcely up-to-date. I noticed one headline in particular:

Fracas in Drung Manager's Office

Louis Dalton said he had a conversation with Moylan in the factory office. He was dissatisfied with Moylan's work and Moylan 'came along and ran at him and beat the face off him with thumps.' Moylan took out a metal drawer and tried to hit him with it and Moylan knocked the phone out of his hand. Witness denied that he had abused Moylan or that he had referred to the employees as 'a crowd of animals in a field.'

I knew that this difference would be resolved by now. Moylan would be reinstated, possibly as foreman, and Louis Dalton would want to make up lost wages but Moylan would insist on working free until all the damage was paid for.

Leaving the papers aside I went to the window, wondering if they had attended the famous wedding in the Seaview Hotel. The window was streaming with rain and I could scarcely see across the street. Nevertheless I continued to gaze out and it seemed to me that I heard, albeit very faintly, over the roofs of the ruined Northern city, a music of guitars and tambourines.

MICHAEL FOLEY

The Stranger

1976

IT WAS a time of great activity in the town. The 'Flower of the West' Festival was about to begin and the citizens were busy with preparations. Fresh bunting and streamers were going up, tradesmen were fussing over displays and a noisy loud-speaker van was touring the streets. Those with nothing to do congregated outside the 'Flower of the West' offices.

So it was that no one noticed a strange arrival at the station. The train had been standing for some time and the sole first-class traveller was leaning back in his seat smoking a cigar. Two things happened almost at once. The loudspeaker van swept by the station advertising the festival, and the train be-gan to pull out of the station. On hearing the announcements the man at once became alert and jumped to his feet. A look of great excitement came on his face and he flung away his half-finished cigar. Then he began seizing items of baggage and throwing them out of the window. When this was com-pleted he opened the door, braced himself (for the train was now moving at speed) and jumped out on to the platform, falling and rolling over several times before climbing to his feet, breathless but apparently unhurt.

This was the man who came to be known as The Stranger.

Some time later he was seen at the reception in the Com-mercial Hotel. He was interested in the Festival, he would like a room overlooking the square. All were intrigued by this eccentric, dressed in a tweed suit and heavy cape, looking for all the world like an English gentleman of some forty years earlier, his luggage consisting of a large suitcase, an empty wooden bird cage and what appeared to be an enormous leather rifle case.

'That's a brave day now,' Con O'Neill, the owner, attempted conversation. The Stranger did not reply.

'Ye'll not find much to shoot around here,' Con pursued, glancing suggestively at the case. The Stranger looked at him and gave a short harsh laugh. Then he went to his room, refusing to let anyone touch either the cage or the case.

News of The Stranger spread swiftly and his comings and goings were widely reported. In the course of the evening he was seen in the Athletic Bar, Owney Martin's, The American Bar, Hugh's Bar, the XL, and The Shamrock Lodge. Finally he turned up once more in the Commercial Hotel which boasted the finest lounge in the town. This was where the business community met, men like James 'Oregon' Duffy, Big Bendy, the garage owner, and Myley Conaghan, the grocer and gent's outfitter. These were important people, men with daughters at convent schools and big houses 'out the road.' Yet here, as elsewhere, The Stranger sat alone, rejecting all attempts at conversation. Repulsed and baffled, the regulars fell back on conjecture.

'Maybe he's travelling for something new,' Myley Conaghan suggested. 'Some kind of swanky cigars or something.'

At this point Slabbery Mickey came into the room. This was the town simpleton, so named because of his drooling mouth. His appearance was extreme – tattered clothes, hair brutally shorn and standing on end – but his eyes were shining with excitement at the commotion of the Festival. He came into the centre of the room and looked round with a pleased, expectant air. Jimmy Oregon took this opportunity to approach The Stranger, who was still at a table of his own although the room was now quite crowded.

'Wait till you see this,' he said, giving The Stranger a familiar nudge, 'this is Slabbery Mickey. His mother took him to Sligo once and he ran away and stole three packets of liquorice allsorts out of Woolworths. The judge asked him why he did it and says Mickey, 'Ah needed big money fast.' The judge said his attitude was very distressing and gave him six months. Didn't know he was simple, ye see.'

And Jimmy Oregon placed his hand on The Stranger's shoulder and leaned over him, helpless with laughter. Myley Conaghan was addressing Slabbery Mickey.

'Here Mickey, give us a bit of French. Come on.'

'Hokey bokey. Hokey bokey cokey.'

'Good man, Mickey. And what about a bit of Spanish?'

'Atty batty watty. Batty atty watty.'

Mickey beamed with pride and there was applause from the little group at the bar and from others who were being drawn into the spectacle. Aware of an audience, Myley jumped to his feet and, catching Mickey by the shoulder, addressed those watching.

'Now Mickey's going to lift the bar – aren't ye, Mickey?' This was Mickey's speciality. He nodded eagerly and crouched down on the floor, putting one arm round each side of the bar. Then he began to strain, grimacing with effort, veins standing out on his forehead, sweat running down his face in streams. The bar did not move but Mickey's arms gradually moved up to shouts of 'Rise her up, Mickey' and 'Good man yourself.' Eventually his arms reached the top and he left off, panting happily.

'Good on ye, Mickey!'

'Sound man!'

Everyone was watching now and The Stranger had full attention when he rose and walked to the bar.

'Michael needs a drink.' This was taken as a witticism and there were loud cries of agreement. These died away when The Stranger turned, face white with rage, eyes blazing a look that 'went through ye like a dose of salts' as Myley Conaghan afterwards put it. A drink was quickly poured and presented to an uncertain Mickey.

'And now,' The Stranger turned to Myley, 'I understand you're a gent's outfitter.'

'That's correct, yes.'

'I would say that Michael needs a new suit.' And here he had such difficulty that there were long pauses between each word, 'For the Festival, you know. Italian style B, with pencil legs and cloth-covered buttons.'

Myley's mouth dropped open in amazement. 'A bum-freezer, ye mean?'

The Stranger gripped the bar with white hands.

'I...mean...Italian...Style B. Make...a...note...of...that.'

'Yes...yes,' Myley dithered, patting his pockets hopelessly. Finally someone handed him a scrap of paper and a pen and The Stranger swept from the room leaving behind some minutes of total silence and then the greatest hubbub the Commercial Hotel had ever known.

At around this time it was learned that The Stranger had adopted a mongrel dog, which he had christened Padraig Pearse. Also Sadie the maid discovered that the great rifle case contained not a weapon but several pairs of soiled underpants.

The consternation was greater than ever.

Then a strange thing occured in the Commercial Hotel. Big Bendy was telling Myley Conaghan a good one.

'Wait till you hear the crack, Myley,' he was saying. 'Ye know the eldest boy, a very serious customer, always his nose in a book? Well, I sent him out for a good winter coat. Sent him down to your place and, wait till you hear, didn't the eejit go into the Black Man's by mistake.'

'Oh he wouldn't be the first,' Myley Conaghan was answering, 'Many's a one made the same mistake – sure doesn't it look much the same on the outside.'

But they both fell silent when The Stranger came into the

room in the company of Biddy Keenan. Biddy Keenan was a tinker. She stalked across the room, insolent and disdainful, practically flouting her shawl and rags. The Stranger followed close behind, never taking his eyes from her, ignoring Myley Conaghan who plucked his sleeve and muttered that the suit was 'coming on rightly.'

Everyone fell silent and it was then that the incident occurred. A ragged newsboy, obviously an old enemy of Biddy's, put his head round the door and, cupping his hands to his mouth, shouted as hard as he could.

'Biddy, Biddy,
Wi' the big wooden diddy!'

At once Biddy's hauteur changed to animal rage. She swung round and crouched, baring her teeth in a snarl.

'Get outa that, ye huer's welt,' she screamed and flung an empty bottle with vicious speed. But the urchin was faster still, disappearing long before the bottle burst above the door. At once Biddy recovered her composure, grinning broadly and moving on to a vacant table. The Stranger, who had watched all this with complete calm, at once rushed ahead and held out her seat. While Biddy adjusted her shawl and glared around triumphantly, The Stranger went to the bar for drinks.

'A large whiskey and a Thunderball, please.' Con O'Neill gaped helplessly. 'Gin and port and a dash of lime,' explained The Stranger with great tolerance.

The 'Flower of the West' Festival is primarily a beauty contest. There is a large and growing list of side attractions but the principal feature is the 'Flower of the West' final in the big marquee on the Saturday night. The 'Flower of the West' finalists line up on stage and each is presented by her sponsor, the winner being chosen by popular acclaim, a method bitterly rued by the committe on this occasion.

The only entry restriction is that the Flower's parents must have been born in the west of the country. This leaves a fairly wide range and as well as local girls there are Liverpool Flowers and New York Flowers and Chicago Flowers and so on. It is the custom for the Flowers to present themselves to the people in a motorcade through the town on the Friday before the final. Each car contains one Flower and is boldly marked 'Chicago Flower,' 'Glasgow Flower' or whatever. There is much cheering and honking of horns – it is a fairly informal affair.

On the Friday afternoon of this festival the cars were lining up in the town square when a most peculiar sight was seen. A tractor driven by The Stranger drove up to the end of the procession and pulled in behind a giant Ford Estate draped with a banner inscribed 'Winnipeg Flower.' On the back of the tractor stood Biddy Keenan, dressed as usual except for a huge sash bearing the legend 'The Wild Flower.' This new arrival was greeted with a noisy outburst of clapping and cheering. The Stranger remained at the wheel and gave every sign of joining the motorcade.

The committee were hopelessly divided. Con O'Neill was for cutting him out – he was 'making a reel of the whole thing.' But others were against interference – the parade was for fun, they argued. Any attempt to curtail the fun would rebound on their own heads. They would be accused of 'taking it thick.'

In the end the latter counsel prevailed and The Wild Flower was allowed to take part, which she did in fine style, accompanied by an excited Padraig Pearse and an equally excited Slabbery Mickey, resplendent in his new suit. Several of her children were also there combing the pavements with cardboard boxes, droning 'Any money for de Wild Flower now, any money for de Wild Flower at all.'

But would she enter for the final? This would really make a mockery of the town. A deputation was sent to The Stranger – James 'Oregon' Duffy, Myley Conaghan and Con O'Neill.

They found him adamant. The Wild Flower had a beauty all her own. They might not be able to see this, he was sorry for them if they couldn't – but he for one could see it and would make sure it got a fair chance. He would enter her for the final. After that it was up to the people.

'Ye're makin' a cow's cock o' the whole thing,' shouted 'Oregon' Duffy in a sudden rage. At once Padraig Pearse rushed at his legs barking furiously.

'Easy boy. Down Patrick.' The Stranger was calm, unruffled. 'May I narrate a dream I had some time ago? An intensely personal experience but it may have some relevance here.' And taking Padraig Pearse on his knee he began the following story.

'One night I was working late on some papers when I seemed to hear a whisper 'Come.' I turned round and there appeared a man who motioned to me. I followed him outside where he vanished, though I felt his breathing beside me. I found myself in the woods, wet branches and leaves slapping against my face. I walked till my legs were sore and wet to the knees. Finally we came to a dark round tower. Again I heard the whisper 'Come' and I entered, seeing him before me once more. I looked deep in his eyes and they seemed to reflect all the horrors he had seen in his life.

'Then I heard footsteps and a woman came in. She was poorly dressed and barefoot but her arms were pale and smooth, without a blemish. As I looked at her a happy feeling came over me.

'I must dry your clothes,' she said. They were indeed quite sodden now. Water was oozing out of my shoes. I did as she told me – took off my clothes and gave them to her. We went up a winding staircase and into a room with a vaulted ceiling. Not a ray of light penetrated the darkness.

'This is my bed,' she whispered. And then again 'Good-night.' I tried to detain her but she faded into the air. Then my night became a fairy tale, a lovely golden memory. I was alone. The night was as thick and heavy as velvet. I was exhausted, my knees were shaking. I was in a daze. At last I lay back and fell into a deep sleep.

'In the morning I awoke in my own room. My clothes were at the foot of the bed but they were damp. My shoes were soaked through.'

The Stranger paused for a long time, stroking Padraig Pearse who had fallen asleep in his lap. Then he resumed softly.

'As I now know the man was Slabbery Mickey and the woman was Biddy Keenan.'

The great marquee was crowded to bursting point. The situation was worse at the entrance, hopelessly blocked by scores of new arrivals and by the steady stream to and from the refreshment tent. A band was playing on the stage but few of the huge crowd were listening. All interest was centred on the contest to come and the merits of the finalists were hotly disputed. Feelings were strongest where the Wild Flower was concerned.

She had more supporters than expected, for news of her entry had spread and the last few days had seen a great influx of tinkers coming to support her. This influx had so alarmed the committee that they had considered abandoning the contest altogether. Then they had thought of banning The Wild Flower – but the tinkers would certainly 'rise a row' if she didn't appear.

At last the entrance was closed off and the contest got under way. The finalists took their positions on stage, a special cheer greeting The Wild Flower. The sponsors took it in turns to introduce the Flowers. As usual the language was conventional in the extreme. There was much mention of 'laughing colleens' and of 'rosy red lips' and 'snow white skin.'

This was normally well received but tonight the audience were restless and ill-disposed to conventional praise. In fact the finalists were being discussed in openly physical terms. Some were praised as 'good hoults,' others scorned as 'cauld curts' and the Winnipeg Flower, by all appearances a very serious girl, had been terribly upset by a loud suggestion that there were cobwebs on it.

The committee were of course alarmed by this increasing rowdiness. But it all ceased abruptly when The Stranger rose to speak. It was obvious that, here at least, the emotions were sincere. Indeed his feelings were so intense that he had difficulty in speaking at all. His voice was scarcely above a whisper and yet the silence was so complete that he was clearly heard at the back of the marquee.

His sentiments were as unusual as his manner. He spoke of the beauty of ordinary things, how in the rush and bustle of our lives we tend to undervalue all that is most precious. Rarely do we have time to reflect and often it takes a complete stranger to open our eyes to the beauty around us. In this very town such a beauty existed.

And he told them a moving story – how one day he had gone to the public gardens to see the flowers. There were the 'fat complacent chrysanthemums' and the 'proud, righteous tulips.' He spoke of the beds with their 'well nourished soil' and their 'careful designs' and their 'perfect unbroken ranks' and he told how he had gone out from that garden and seen a single lowly dandelion sprouting from a crack in the pavement. Although it was a crowded thoroughfare he had no choice but to make his feelings known.

'I had no choice,' The Stranger said, 'The terrible poignancy of that flower tore a cry from my lips.'

When he sat down there was silence for a full minute. Then there was uproar. The outcome was certain now – The Wild Flower had it easily. The band came back on and the refreshment tent, entirely empty for so long, was hit by a tidal wave of customers. There was laughter and dancing and the centre of attraction was the triumphant Biddy Keenan. She was 'swizzed' in the centre of the floor by a succession of laughing young men. Then she was carried shoulder high twice around the marquee. Then she was installed on a throne on the stage.

Finally The Stranger was called on for another speech and only then was it discovered that he was nowhere to be seen. No one had seen him leave and a search around the tents revealed nothing. There was a growing uneasiness and an anxious party, headed by Slabbery Mickey, set off for the Commercial Hotel.

What they found was a room with no people or belongings, only a mongrel dog whining and scratching an empty bird cage.

It was some years later. A small group of friends, James 'Oregon' Duffy, Big Brendy and Myley Conaghan were on their way from the Atlantic Bar to the Commercial Hotel. As always they were marvelling at how much had still to be learned about that momentous Festival week. James 'Oregon' Duffy was particularly engrossed, staring at the ground, not taking much part in the conversation, a look of great amazement on his face. Suddenly he stopped them all dead in their tracks and burst out,

'Did yese know Patrick Pearse was a bitch?' Myley and Big Brendy were dumbfounded.

'What was that?'

'What?'

'Padraig Pearse was a bitch. Sadie the maid told me. His mongrel, ye remember. It was a bitch – but he called it Padraig Pearse.'

Big Brendy and Myley were no less amazed.

'I didn't know that now. That's a good one.'

'That's a new one on me too. Boys-a-boys-a-boys.'

And the old friends continued on their way.

Dermot Healy was born in Finea, County Westmeath, Ireland, in 1947. He has lived in Cavan, Dublin, and London, and recently returned to Ireland. He has published poetry and prose in various periodicals. He has received two Hennessy Literary Awards, in 1974, and in 1976. At present, he is working on two contrasting groups of short stories, 'Sciamachy' and 'Poverty of Location.' He is married, and has one child.

The following stories are from 'Sciamachy,' a series of inter-connected, but independent pieces. Sciamachy comes from **Scia**: shadow; and **Machy**: to fight (Greek). Healy sees Sciamachy as fighting with shadows, or shadow boxing; also as fighting with shadows of pretension.

DERMOT HEALY

The Island and the Calves

1977

EASTER WEEK dragged on in the distant crowded church.

By the house too, the spiritual world was ecstatic and sensual. Jim felt he might lose control of each and every moment, deep base music, The Seven Last Words of Jesus Christ on the Cross by Haydn, till ultimate flight and optimism. He had begun to name with awe each part of the outside world, gaining equilibrium. The early turbulence of wind and rain had deepened the reflections in the now calm lake, a sensual pike rose momentarily across the surface, spills appeared under the drying trees in the water. As if small fry were rising. The country Sussex house was packed with prams and children, wet dolls sat out under the birches, cows nudged at their fodder and drifted down to the unblossomed rhododendrums.

In the deep pool of water, the serrated edges of the purple pines sharpened towards sunset.

Winds channelled through the woods with a low hum. The things that my soul refuse to touch are as my sorrowful meat was Edward's cry. Down by the lake's edge Jim and Edward were walking. Edward was dressed like a Jew, woolen hat, scapular like a lanceolate that pierced his breast, and eyes so light a blue that the pupil might slip away, melt. And then the brooding irony of devotion. In him the body and soul were one. The actor's idea of the stage and its dimensions were present in his judgment of things. He had just arrived from Gloucester, thence from a further coastline where he and some friends had celebrated the real mass on a deserted beach. The priest (Jim had strode alongside him at a workers' march in London, his Scottish voice haranguing, more then then most, the slogans) was a social worker, the altar girls had tended to him, they craved poverty and the expression of their bodies, how you might never trust a crucifix, the Temple and the Holy Ghost were different but not too different, and Edward's speech concerned otherness and celebration.

They walked on Jim's land.

The figure of the young priest, as a ghost of modernity, walked between them.

By the flush of leaves and waves coming together, apart, on the shore.

Why could Jim only now and then turn to his friend to look into his transparent eyes, what was the presence that confronted them, the one that bore them apart? Let that otherness then bear Witness.

For it would be unfair to show how much they loved each other, that would be to invade them; let their occupations this day speak for them.

Besides the odd human detail. They have, for old times sake, erected an aerial off a high tree to pick up the mass in Irish from Radio Eireann, to allow the chants from Jim's home country to permeate the house. A minute's silence here is worth hours somewhere else in a year's time. The preciousness of this turbulence that is not fleeting. Not magic, but possession of something between the rhododendrums and the Birch. Young willows flock in the hedges, the catkins have sprung furry with yellow combs. Edward will not listen or look at the trees or the water, all these images, the geranium and the lily have gone within, he has an ambiguous response to man's delight in nature, yet his ecstasy is not shortlived.

Jim burns with the necessity to get things done, a busy self, he perches on the shoulder of his friend looking at the competing world.

The house and the kitchen were wrecked by the chaotic

night before, the children stepped over and added to the debris, babies crawled into cupboards, and a neighbour's child was studying the contents of a cardboard waste box. A young girl sat outside eating sand. Beside her, a crisp bag filled to bursting with primroses, thorns, pismires. So after their silent walk the men set to work. That is, Jim washed and scrubbed the kitchen down while Edward talked with hardly creditable gestures, or hardly heard what his friend answered, such was his zealous discovery of spiritual energy. He swaggered between the windows and the trees with chopped timber for a fire that was not burning. Popped large lumps of apple tart into his mouth. The radio was switched off during the priest's passionate ritual for the burial of Christ. The timorous martyrdom that crackled through space. In the silence came the sound of oars beating off a boat across the waters. A hare with long girl's thighs and legs stopped short of Jim in the garden.

He appraised the tension trembling in the hare's back, the jump withheld in the sockets of his knees; Jim had interrupted a joyous fling around the wild apple trees.

They looked at each and sauntered off to their various retreats.

Margaret was upstairs sleeping, tired from going to and fro in the earth, and from walking up and down in it. Last night, she had screamed, Pain is practical, it's not something you go on and on with. For the men put no trust in their intelligence, expecting only to create well.

Now, today, she had been regretful, knowing how easy it is to inflict the truth on others without considering its possible repercussions on oneself. She listened to the two men downstairs, doubted her heroic capabilities, leaves sparkled on the walls around her. Haydn's music burst through into the final celebration. She was glad that the children had not surrendered to their conciliatory fathers, that she could read continually up here with emphasis.

Each morsel of food made her grow lightheaded. Her hair drifted across the pillow, her skin dried.

Under the boardwalk, down by the sea, Edward was singing in a mock-Oxford accent for the barely interested children.

Jim listened doubtfully.

Now darkness. The much blessed body had been buried under the monolith of ritual, and so Edward brings his Bible in from the car. The coot and the sky-goat blow their horns over the purple lake. Closing the door, the inmates of the house, the trapped butterfly and sleeping robin under the rafters, all heard the sudden mad screech of the geese rising with a chorus of screams, the lake suddenly fell sideways as they flew off. Emigration had begun. Edward read from the Old Testament, from Job and then from the Song of Songs, from the Natural Law in the Spiritual World, the everlasting kissing and fondling, how sweet the hooves of the doe. While Jim (was it just taking the most innocuous view?) imagined a priest in sleeveless leather donkey jacket mounting the marble steps, where biblical vegetation was trapped, charcoal dirt on his arms, and then erratic improvisations in the organ loft.

The Song of Songs was Edward's place in time.

For him there was no need of externalising the presence of God.

That was Edward's totality.

Yet, there remained the music of the ballet, unprecedented, without such dancers, the song of the heart. For Jim it had begun this way. He had followed the movements of the calves for no special reason, other than after wet nights when the wind ranged heavily, he would find them in different places under the hedges. Their farmer provided fodder for their travels. From the general sheet of cold he surmised that the wind one day came from the East. It drove manfully against the wall of the house, repeated itself in dreams, was present in water and in the ruddy veins of the child.

The calves were tucked in against the further ditch of the field. So that, too, was East for them, the nebula. Towards the Stones of the Dogs mountains, under the plural form of myths, they had found refuge. During the night and the following day, rain fell harshly and at noon the wind softened, warmth resurrected, and he surmised from the South the wind came, it softened the eyes, the hair of Margaret, cooled the bushes...the calves were now under the ash-and-willow hedge to the left of the unattended Holly Well; hiding from the warm bucketing wind, chopping, straying, pondering, the flaming calf in the lead, all the rest mottled black and white.

Always one stood, while the others rested their chilled hooves, stared unblinkingly at all who passed.

Now Jim knew the four points of the compass from the wind and the calves, the corners of that elementary field he extended, onto the lake to find direction from there. For then there were no books in the house, no radio with which to guide him. And what was permanent, what stood still, would always point in a different direction to the man or the bird always moving, recognising and turning, lifted on a current of air. He moved the field mentally out onto the water, between those lines of white surf, sallied forth with those earthly calves onto the rushing waves for North, South, East, and West.

And even though this was an emotional, fundamental fashion of discovery, yet when the wind died down (no west wind ever blew) and passion departed, when passion departed and reason returned, to the branches of a tree separating the heavens and the earth, when he stood bewildered by the strange simplicity of the sorrowful day that follows the joyous day, when man's heart might take that agile journey towards always discovering anew, still the points of that compass held firm.

The edges ran sharply out onto the murky headlands, over

beautiful, distressed places, tapered off on mountain peaks and toppled palings on hawk and pine heads, beyond what he could not get to the other side of, remaining here, always imagining.

Now for Edward, he places the field on an island, though in a further lake. It took this sunshine, calm waters and relentless perception. He boated out to the island, drew a map of it, the monastery walls, the nest of the Heron was East, when his plan was finally completed. In a line east from the house on this particular day you had the red calf, the Birch, the aerial, the hawk, the heron. Fossils he collected for charms, as in older times; the knowledge of structure went undisturbed. The purple of the waves stained their arms. History became the study of disappearing softness, for hardness always remained, the most accessible material of Man.

Here on the island he experienced the distance between the island and the field, the pleasure of nesting in the warmest part, like the calves. Where all brilliant stones have been sketched upon by the bones of fish, shells of mollusc, cups of coral, the brains of kings and labourer. This Island, morning receiver of gifts, plants and water, up where dawn's light has slipped from its chilled moorings and drifts among the tall heads of the spruces, where the herons are babbing, and where the deer once slept with his nose on his tail, closer to the Word, and no closer for all that energy spent.

The children screamed to be allowed on board, maddened by Jim oaring so constantly, seeking relief between home and the island, his pockets weighed down by stones, his hearing half-gone from the warfare of startled birds.

His house that day took on more and more the appearence of an abandoned novel, the children and he and Margaret could no longer sustain any kind of order. For at last he had authenticated the outside world, and each part was now sustained by itself and no longer needed a deity nor an interpreter. Such wanderings are approved of for a time, no matter their exaction of practicality from the innovators' lives, if they do not become bitter or flaunt their discoveries, like the apostles, like myths, before a tiring, believable audience. Into this house, then, as Margaret came down the stairs for a light supper, and the geese beat their way off into the appointed direction, Edward trustingly brought his Bible, sought solace, and then, unprompted and sonorously, began his reading of the Song of Songs.

DERMOT HEALY

Jude and his Mother

1977

I DREAMED that life-energy itself could be siphoned off at the moment before death. There is nothing unusual in that dreamlike speculation, a refusal to harden the arteries, you might think, common or garden science fiction. But in the dream this life is then contained with the maximum of pleasure on the shiny surface of a penny piece, and eternalised by the coin spinning on the head of a fragile matchstick. These matchsticks (for there were other lives there spinning around besides my evidently doubtful one) moved pleasantly backwards and forwards on a thin plank in a small bedroom, the plank balanced on I know not what, but sustaining this planetary motion, these shiny, commercial, spinning surfaces.

If you wanted to put the picture into a frame, on a penny, analyse this dream in the deterministic fashion of our contemporary analysts, you might say it was caused by a mild reading of our Marxist masters, or being a Jungian, care to think that this was the way all life was planned, at least for me. You could speak of my debts and my guilt. And the aesthetic mortification of man being so reduced, but, then, can I afford to have you in my dreams?

I don't live in a relaxed regime, I'm afraid.

Not that I am dissatisfied or under pressure, I too have had my moments of joy, when the bar was cleared for the rasp of the fiddle and the songs of Marcus Sommerville, my mother's songster. But order, though I might desire it, became the great tragedy. Nor do I mean the vacuum that instinct might fill. I did not want to fill my life with decadence and indolent learning, the pastiche of Europe. Nor make a hero of my neurotic, cockless self. I preferred the political truth at this time to the musical traditional proverbs of my mother. Not the German psyche, the Andalusian colour, and yet all of these. Perhaps it was merely justifying and activating my presence in life at a given moment, by searching for a further consciousness than that which is called subconscious, and that which is called conscious. I began to plan my dreams, decide when to wake from them.

What remained after I had completed these exercises, sometimes with success but more often with fear, was that my evaluation of life did not comply with what I had hoped for. I believed I was lying, or had merely believed I was planning my dreams. This doubt became the real subconscious, the third event of my mind, which I could not control or dismiss, but only continue to gather evidences, both positive and negative and doubtful, doubtful being the category that supplied my impetus and love.

It was I, then, who put my Imperial head on the coin, I who woke spontaneously in my bedroom, and I who must discharge my duties.

But the rushing in to help someone has a strange history. To be effective it must be over in seconds, and to remain integral it must never be mentioned. I gathered that political evangelists are a bore in the intellectual sphere, yet still intellectuals are desirous of freedom of content. The status No. On the other hand, those who take an active interest in our political life and do not forego aesthetics, find the combination hard to maintain, or so tradition has it. But often upset at night, when sleep was not imparted to me readily due to an imaginary illness or a heavy cold...like a brick lodged in the centre of my chest, its cold edges resting on my lungs...I would lift up a translation of Marx and feel restored by that sense of colossal empty strength in the world.

The long day's drink was a cultural hardship, it happened so often.

My feet unhinged, and my mind too.

Decadence : *decline of art due to a pronounced depletion of vital energies, resulting in the rejection of practical life in favour of the composure of contemplation; an aesthetic fear or glorification of action; an unnecessary martyrdom; a lack of will to live without contradictions; pessimism.*

Anyway, for romantic reasons, I chose to work with my body because of its liberating effect, but this therapy only lasts for a while, becomes an excuse for boasting (craftsmen are the energy cycle for capitalists and socialists), no matter how often you conjecture or explain its necessities to others.

Beating the ends of rubber mats wears you down. The supervisor follows me around like a pal, because of my education; we stand on the floor looking up at the spacious offices, debating our future. He makes sure I receive slight jobs, brings my cup of tea with his to a separate table in the canteen, jousts, prowls, is mischievous. The factory is near Woodgreen, opposite the bookies, a grey half mile from the Underground. I stand by my own furnace, clamp down the shape of the toilet bowl, the rubber recoils under the heavy heat, my great gloves hold the flame. Keep the clamp in position, lean on it, the machine shivers, and then I withdraw the design. The burnt rubber is doused with water. The ends cut off with a knife. The threads inspected. Sometimes they hang askew, as when the strings of a harp are held aside to permit the passage of a sweeter note. Pop music is played all day, the supervisor remembers the happier tunes of Music While You Work. The walls and galvanised roofs burn, and the ladies love to daunder in the cooler air of the finishing evening, hesitate within the gates a minute longer than necessary to facilitate a more blissful entrance into the humid streets.

Scorched clothes leave behind welts of the appearance of bed sores, as if today we turned and turned and walked the factory floor but could not find solace.

The girls have forgotten the callisthenic optimism of their past, eye makeup and diesel darken their lids, they are exuberant, sexual, joking, tired-flesh makes a problem for the future. But unlike Wagner, they cannot stroke satin till the mood comes. His roughish gramarye. They expel their ghosts with lavish foreplay, as Li Ho has written

> *If Heaven too had passions*
> *Even Heaven would grow old.*

I will never really enter their lives unless I marry one of the girls or join their union. Either way, it will be something to do with joining, but not dedication. Take Josu now, how more and more he desired privacy, changed groups, attacked from a different angle our youth. So that for us, growing older, maturing, will never come as a surprise. But after our first whole hearted hatred mellowed, it was not his desire that broke down, not his desire for companionship, it was more the strain that we, those closest to him, exerted. We suspected some falsehood, it was at our fingertips, but then it became apparent that life itself directs the course of error and truth. We, as individuals, were not so privileged. 'Jude,' said my abstemious mother, 'You waste your time diluting truth with words.' She is big and fat in the manner of many women from our district, and lords over her cattle, eternally soured by the society in town, which thrives because of its elitist momentum. The great social endeavours there sustain the lonely and the ambitious by their collaboration. It is of no use to mention to her such clichés as Urban Renewal or Machinery of Man. The despair of wanting to go someplace to be taken in. Political excesses. 'Today,' she says, 'a country lad knows more about machinery, electricity, plumbing, and animals then his city counterpart. His awkward stance is technically sure.' All deteriorations and crookedness are commonplace, and to speak of them with Puritan disdain to her, is to speak of the obvious, things have changed, such observations have lost their original critical vitality, they just add to the nervous gestures of my mother's chin. January 31st found me back in the village arguing with her. We called on her brother, the shopkeeper. Business was failing, his sweetjars were half empty, musty sugar filled the glass. The wooden till was full of coins only, the rashers on the counter weeping. 'I always associate such business with terror,' she remarked to him, 'The fear of being unable to deal with the public.'

'If you hadn't the money you might be off to the Home,' he said, seeking sympathy.

'Unless your marbles are unsettled, anyone that would burn you for a fool would have wise ashes.'

'As long as I had millions,' he answered, knocking his hand off his fist.

'The poor auld fuck,' she said as we strolled home, though she felt sad for him, and taunted him wisely. In the morning I went into the field to perform my ablutions. Cold human shits in the back garden, dotted along the tangled hedge, the yellow frozen toilet paper sparkling with frost. A bird flew out from an empty place left by a missing slate in the roof. The kitchen windows were lit by winter flower patterns; sharp edges of transparent leaves lasted till midday. Reflections fossilized. Crude radio plays she turned up high, written with frantic characterizations that border on embarrassment.

The tips of the fingers disappeared from walking abroad.

Oh, my mother was not secured by religious sanction against outrage! She had been flattened at the crossroads. Everyone at first supported the stone throwing because of her tongue and later extended it by extremism and constance or redeemed it by prayer and power. The Passion of Christ was the local impotence. The bearded man who had demeaned her and loved her, was fattened by and exasperated by the cold, undignified clay. 'Humbleness is not good enough' was one of her generalizations. She so cherished the spring, in this, her little island of thought. We rocked to the laughter of my dead father's funny stories repeated in the kitchen, the two of us, after tea. How they'd, his friends and him, tied an ass to the door on Halloween night, and twice, the knocker had sounded, she answered and saw no one; the third time, pulling hard at the door she drew the curious donkey into the hall. A bird-scuffle over her head, while kneeling she beats cloth of stone. The distant and sudden argument of nature, but 'Jude,' she says, 'one has to learn not to grieve over futile arguments.' Knowing that my fantasies cannot screen off nor add to the appearance of the future. For dialogue but satisfies my urge to communicate mostly in retrospect. Belligerent in public, working in secret, that the critic in me might chose or invent realities that the fatalist in me absolves. Rain dropping on the hot sands of the White City dogtrack. In the village the smell of burning feathers. Yeats sign.

Lorries and water go everywhere.

Being there or here, holidays or arguments never seem to end for me. A passage of time here, there, or hereafter, repeats itself either venomously or joyously. So I remarked to Anna as we passed by a drunk on the Underground, deliriously intimating some secret in his inside pocket. We were carrying a fluorescent tube and a bag of torn material which we'd found in cardboard boxes outside a city design centre. Anna had tried their various colours and shapes in the train, each oddment is a decoration eventually. The drunk is black-faced, vulnerable bags under his brown eyes, wearing a red and blue light-woollen scarf. An Indian scapular hangs from his pockmarked throat. He took out a photograph from his untidy wallet and looked longingly at it. Then he struck his head off a pillar a number of times.

Quickly sand was poured over his vomit and two cops carried him out of the Underground, laughing to each other, intimates, his feet dragging, roar of the train. 'He's O.K.' I said to Anna but she threw me a spiteful look which I returned. Each drunk in a cell is a world onto a world.

At the meeting, the sound of the speaker's voice was drowned out by engine after engine, only his hands carried the momentum of his heart. He uses a mixture of wit, criticism and bravery, his thoughts strain under the skin of his temple. I mean his face exaggerates the quality of his mind. We are there, complete with fluorescent tube, to interrupt the meeting and disparage his reasoning. Anna has a formidable weapon which issues a sound like a foghorn. Jim, from the Industrial North, is urgent and versatile with his declamations. An egotist, he lacks pity and judgement, but with a spiritual flourish of his country boots he stands some seven inches above any other man in the room. He gains equilibrium from the cottage he lives in, in Sussex, with his tumultuous family. But Josu, the speaker, is unruffled. Aesthetics and adolescence were laws he had long ago dispensed with, though the young Spaniards mock him, he indulges in highminded caprices.

'It's the man on the street, they fear' he remarked.

'Whose rhyme shall we use tonight? What word will break into a thousand recognizable pieces to suit their etymological backgrounds, the need of purity? Do you even know what I mean?'

After leaving the ill attended meeting, we went onto the streets singing our hoarse European songs.

Though later, discouraged, when Anna and I sat talking in the darkness, she said 'We may be twice as romantic as we think; when there was no politics to suit us well we went out and invented a form of our own.' 'That's optimism,' I said, and we laughed. But could tell the distance from danger and practicality. We were just middle-class would-be intellectuals down on our luck. This led to further discussion and cruelty between us. The raucous throb of cars and machines communicated in the planks of the shanty, buildings were coming down, staccato explosions from the industrial estate filled the night, and later the swearing of the street dancers. From the other rooms, the most humane and compassionate case against revolution...the passionate longing for solitude and silence.

And as always, Anna watches me as I read (perhaps as Josu once watched her), looking up difficult words with patient, annoying care, interrogating the dictionary, and sometimes arriving at the same word time and time again, as if it could not rest on my palate, its strangeness a world I could not enter with my senses or experience, needing Beckett's brisk nihilism, by its history a novel built round an attitude till the dictionary becomes The Book of Revelations. For truly no other fiction could capture my mind so.

Revelation? Fiction? Yea, sweet God, for no word could ever settle on a meaning, unless an arbitrary one. Here then, among the rich verbs and frugal nouns, the workers of the tongue, my first course in Dialectics. The Historical Imagination gives us something vital and lethal, I once read. Till Nothingness is hostile and treacherous. And terminology is not an exact science for Anna either, she too favours my mother's generalizations and their attended ultimates and contradictions.

Of terminology: 'Anything so generous with meaning, with actual principles, with indisputable laws, can provide you with a platform, a stand, whenever you so desire' she says ironically, betraying no sympathy towards man's weakness for equality or authority.

We had everything at our fingertips, but could not find the truth.

So when Mary, Queens of Scots, died, she endured two strokes of the executioner's axe 'making very smale nayse or none at all.' This I read in the British Museum one summer's day. Her little dog had crept under her clothes, emerged after the execution and could not be gotten forth by force, would not depart from the dismembered corpse but lay between her head and shoulders. So Anna's head lies between my heart and soul. Her art has the capacity to look at itself and society at the same time. The shift to modernity, I mean her passage across the earth, has wrenched her eyes from inwardness, harsh tempers occupy the vacuum created, and her body is as alive as the heart, both joyful and sorrowful, of that Royal dog. She does not recognize me either upon wakening or going to sleep. She is not an exile from, but champions Conscience, the effort of will.

The owning of Knowledge and nothing more.

I longed for the warmth between us to return, but too long has been spent in interpretation without the satisfaction of creation.

How human that our plot should entertain!

On the island we fought because of my jealousy. Perhaps, too, I was aware that it was her gift bringing me there. She flirted with the barboy who was chewing the seal of a wine bottle, his motor-cycle helmet gleaming at the end of the bar. His age was indeterminable, about 38 or 39, greyhaired, bluebearded, with humorous eyes. I had lost her earlier and now found her coaxing him towards intimacy. In one hand she held a cold jug of wine, in the other, his. Somewhere a mouth organ was playing on the summer evening. The gratuitous life where caution stops. The argument continued out into the warm air where soon it would be suddenly cold. We beat each other fervently. Later, he came on his bike behind us, pulled up and picked her out of the warm dust. Goats bleated from the trees above our heads, upset by the performance. He took both of our reluctant hands and joined them, he spoke fluently in Spanish till we reached our wooden chalet perched among the hot blue mountains. He followed our car with outlandish gesticulations. Every violence is a restitution, then, consummated often among friends. He drank with us, we had wine from the French Quarter. This man's slight figure hung over the shady-brown valley through the unaccustomed windows till dawn. For nowhere in that land did windows open outward, but inward onto the fountains. His predicament? He only stood in for washing bottles very seldom. He had been looking for light work ever since the war. To protest without being named is useless. How you, Anna, sat on your bed questioning. Our total happiness there as we watched the lights twinkle on the mainland. Crude is my shape, her scalpel sharp. And any reality is only appraised by its followers and each ideal demolished by self-justification. The giver, then, and the receiver are equal. The female blackbirds twittered and whistled across the fields. Impulsive actions do not lead to a man of strong will. And when I return from Anna to my mother and use her house as a battle-ground for my frustrations, to accelerate her nervous devotion to truth, is this not again my Infancy? How will it be, say, in twenty years time, when I return home some January to sit by her kitchen windows, where the coltsfoot is bracing itself and the slender spur of the wood-violet is hardening, and know I have failed. Because I will be either powerful or humane. When tottering back from her brother, the shopkeeper's shop, I told my mother of this conceit; she dropped her hands in dismay and turned to me exasperated. 'What will you do for that side of the house-' she asked, 'You speak with the self-analysis of an author for whom all things are planned.' For her, clerks, authors, are the guardians of the permanent, corrupted human nature. She would never leave her statements in the hands, in the gesture of an artist. What could I do? We don't all feel our lives are a loss, she was hinting, turning round, affectionate for a moment.

'Begin again, my sweet, begin again' she said, matron of virility, not some sweetness introduced into the masculine but beauty with strength, its existence previously in the world and now in harmony with it, favoured by unfrightened youth. The reverse of the coin.

Desmond Hogan was born 1951 in Ballinasloe, County Galway, Ireland. At the age of seventeen, he turned down a four year scholarship to study art, because he wanted to continue writing. He won a Hennessy Literary Award in 1971, the first year this prize was given. His short stories have appeared widely in Ireland and the United Kingdom; two of his plays were produced at the Abbey Theatre in Dublin, and one on radio. His first novel, 'The Ikon Maker,' (Irish Writers' Cooperative, 1976) was a best seller in Ireland. His work has been translated into German and Polish. He has completed a second novel, and is now working on a third.

DESMOND HOGAN

Mothers of Children

THEIR FLAT lay alongside the canal; it was pretty to watch the skies pale as Chinese napkins and observe swans in flight. Denise watched her child grow; his body straight as a pin and his hair the colour of wrought copper. A woman who looked no more than fifteen or sixteen, she drew social assistance while her husband provided irregular payments. Dorine, on the other hand, was often bereft. Her husband, a rich South of England man, drowsed on his mother's estate in Kent, sniffing cocaine and, if he wasn't too distracted by young women, remembering his anarchist days in Dublin, days of street theatre and nude flights into the Irish sea on moon-struck beaches. Dorine fed her daughter Lara with as much care as Denise. Diet in the canal-side flat could often be mistaken to consist totally of honey, soya beans and brown munchy bread from Bewleys. Dorine had replaced a girl whose lover had died from barbiturates and whose silhouette could often be seen flitting down by the canal, face washed pale as the porridge the children left after them in the mornings, hair still sparkling and red.

Dorine would spy her out the window. 'Here comes the Blessed Virgin,' she'd say. The girl would never stop, walk on as though she'd never lived here, greatly to Denise's chagrin. She'd liked and even loved this girl; she'd tended her as she tended her son. But the girl's lover had died; his mother had died a year before, a noted cookery expert on Irish radio, and the girl broke up and left.

So Dorine had moved in, replete with baggage from a

previous seedy flat. It was pleasant here and there were patterns of swallows on the curtains and a view of the canal and a shop that looked about to crumble next door. Bliss was the first word that came to her head. She'd known Denise well for years. Denise had even made love to her husband, but all slights had been forgiven after both women had spent a while in a Krishna Murti commune in the South of England.

> *'It has to be found from moment to moment, in the smile, in the tear, under the dead leaf, in the Vagrant thoughts, in the fullness of love.'*

This quotation from Krishna Murti was to be found on many of Dorine's books; one had only to open the Book of Common Prayer or *The Female Eunuch* to see it. In the weeks after Dorine had moved in she got odd jobs in fashion shops off Stephen's Green, holding the fortress as velvet clothed owners paraded up and down Grafton Street.

Denise minded the children for these periods while Dorine minded the offsprings in evenings when Denise, intent on poetry, wandered down Grafton Street, sidling into pubs where poets wandered in and out, one wearing a skirt, with grey hair thrown back like John the Baptist. She'd have cider and speak to plump female folk singers or to sexually repressed eighteen year olds or to blond bar-men who were reputedly bi-sexual.

Grafton Street was indeed a temptation especially as spring burst, reaching forbidden heights in the sky; purple and red patches were to be seen. It was as though the city had thrown off its clothes; her youth rose, early marriage, handsome faces, young men in white trousers in the South of England. Her marriage, a fine point in her life, had broken up irreparably. She'd been contented to a new virginity. Her child grew like an apple-blossom, burgeoning to a fine-pointed apple. The city was almost enough for her, its ancient graces and sombre statues. Loneliness crossed her mind that spring, but she flicked it away; loneliness was gone and a more passionate self presented itself to her; inside she was as a seamstress of fine moments and as such began a platonic relationship with a rather Rilkean young man who wrote beautifully and for the moment was without his lady-friend, who had disappeared to foreign parts.

On seeing Denise enjoy these moments, Dorine engaged in a few affairs; she began sleeping around.

One young man drove her off to Galway one weekend in his van and they cavorted on a bed beside the docks.

She returned wearing a long black dress, one strap falling on her powder pale arms.

Denise looked still.

Silence pervaded; Dorine had broken an unwritten law.

Dorine registered the rebuke, ceased seeing young men, engaged in a new look, walking up and down Grafton Street with a look that would have done Yeats proud at his most lonesome and inspired moments.

During this time their children accepted something of the same serenity.

Denise's child began writing one line poems about cherry blossoms.

Dorine's daughter spoke in highly articulate phrases to strangers about swans.

Visitors came; they saw the locks of heather in jam-jars, the crosses woven with designs.

One man who lived in the Wicklow mountains with a pin struck through his nose came often; he came early, as he was barred from most pubs in town. At one stage he was undergoing a Cuchullain phase, imagining himself to be the legendary hero and had a professional photographer come to Wicklow to photograph him in a tunic.

Now he practised Satanic rites and had enigmatic signs painted on his nostrils.

In Denise's or Dorine's company, however, he was calm and merely drank tea.

In these weeks Dorine and Denise became closely associated with one another, firstly as mothers of children, secondly as eccentrics. Dublin is a city which desires nothing more than to squash individuality; one must belong to a lesbian group or a Marxist group or an arts circle. Denise and Dorine drifted alone.

Their times in the pubs were irregular. Their features were often confusing. They'd begun to look like one another.

So people suspected them. People whispered 'lesbian,' 'whore,' 'bitch.'

Denise and Dorine braved it all.

Sometimes they'd sit at home and discuss their pasts; Denise had been the rich offspring and married beneath her, Dorine had married way above her slum origins. Both now had an equal share of what some might consider bourgeois mannerisms, but what others might connect with Rilke, Yeats, Virginia Woolf.

In a city of sick and small minds they were individualistic to a core.

The young man whom Denise was seeing would often come to see them. He was mourning his lover, lost for the moment; the girls felt a sense of urgency about him, quickly made him peppermint tea when he appeared.

For his benefit they stuck a saying from Goethe on the wall: 'Trust yourself.'

He was in need of repair after his girl-friend left him, so the girls would often cook for him, pick up old jumpers for him, or listen to him talk.

He was a cause as much as Vietnam used be a cause, his spirit must not be allowed to flag, so they often discussed him, ways of attracting his girl-friend back.

'She's with Jesus people in California.'

'That's it then.'

'What?'

'It's over.'

'The Lord is more powering than the flesh.'

'Yes.'

But eventually the possibility that love was dead frightened them. Both girls wandered off alone on different nights, and neither would admit they were seeking, however vaguely, lovers.

Their two children were sleeping together now and they themselves were sleeping partners, each in sleek nightdresses like miniature Ophelias, miniature because they were both so small.

Denise had begun shaping poems which were published in Dublin broadsheets, and Dorine was making embroidered dresses which were quickly sold in the Dandelion Market. A sense of independence had arrived, and one day a reporter from the Irish Press came to interview Denise.

She expounded on marriage and men while Dorine looked on approvingly. Dorine had begun wearing glasses now, and Denise resurrected an old pair of her own.

April had sidled over and these were the first days of May with budding water-lilies among the old tyres of the canal.

They were sleeping closer to one another, and then it was heard that the blond bi-sexual bar-man was getting married to a professor at the university, while the Rilkean boy had a homosexual affair with an American film producer who had come to film a love-story set against the background of 1916.

The world had gone mad. One night they attempted to make love; it didn't work. They stared at one another sadly and forlornly and kept their distance.

Dorine's little girl had fallen in love with the abusive son of a doctor who lived around the corner and cycled by on a brash tricycle.

Denise's son had begun quoting Chinese verse which his father taught him at weekends.

A social welfare officer visited them who thought he was in a lunatic asylum, Buddah, Krishna Murti, Goethe rolled into one on the walls and sex manuals on the floor. He quickly left, raised Denise's weekly income, and secured social security benefits for Dorine, who hadn't had them before.

Denise stared out the window. She realized something had gone wrong. She went home to her mother for a week. Her mother, an alcoholic, was cousin to a government minister.

She stared at Denise.

'All artists must go,' she said, 'That's the way it's been and always will be. The Irish will not recognize their own kind.'

Dorine was re-emerging into a world of squalid sex; one day she found her daughter in the back yard on top of another child, this time from the slums across the canal.

She sat in the kitchen and began crying. She knew it would take an immense effort to rise above the squalor of this city, she knew she'd have to grow in a way Krishna Murti and Goethe had long ago directed her.

That would be difficult!

Denise returned and said she was leaving. The two women looked at one another. Dorine was reminded of the Black Madonna of Dublin in Whitefriar Street church, a resigned but omnipotent look.

Denise was struck by Dorine's beauty, her short blonde hair. It was no use, this city which spread about them was squeezing them in, this city of brash and boldly coloured boutiques, this city of night-clubs where you got salacious cherry-topped ice creams, this city scarce in pennies and scarce in hope.

'Where are you going?'

'London.'

Dorine reminded Denise that both had had hard times in London; they'd left Ireland once with their individual husbands and lived there.

If it hadn't been for the kindness of fruit and vegetable

dealers in Picadilly they wouldn't have survived. 'I'll go further,' Denise said, 'Maybe to France.' Dorine was wearing glasses and spoke intellectually about Joyce. Ireland devours her own, she said, it hadn't changed since Joyce's daughter was flying off her head in Zurich or Joyce was inscribing the last ornate words of *Ulysses* in Paris.

It was an admission difficult for Denise; she'd grown much over the last months, she had not made love once, she'd resisted the offers of painters exhibiting in the Project Arts Centre. She went walking that night and met the boy whose girl-friend had left him on O'Connell Bridge. He smiled. She quickly discovered there'd been no homosexual affair. In his own way he was attempting to grow inwardly without the attentions of sycophants. They retired to a cafe and there had a meal, eating attentively. Both agreed they'd been very happy in their early twenties, the boy with his blond furry-haired girl, Denise with white trousered young men who studied Krishna Murti on green lawns in the South of England. Such happiness was not confined to any period in one's life, they both agreed, such happiness was one's heritage from childhood and had to grow, tended carefully by intuitive and attentive minds.

They kissed on parting that night.

Some months later, Dorine grown a little older and a little lonelier, and living in another part of Dublin received a post-card from Denise. It was from Menton in the South of France, where Denise was living with a painter.

She was writing a lot; she remarked that Katherine Mansfield, the New Zealand short story writer, had once inhabited a house nearby; she remarked that here spring was always imminent, and that the sea was blue. Dorine fingered the card, recalling Denise after she'd returned from seeing that boy in June. Dorine had made her tea with one spoon of honey in it, and as she'd handed it to her, she'd noticed Denise staring at the window.

She'd known then Denise's moment was at hand. The evening had been deep and Dorine had worn a lilac dress, and as Denise had sipped her tea she'd whispered 'It's hard. Nothing comes easy.'

It was winter now. Again the sky was heavy outside. Dorine fingered the card, she wished to tear the blossom from the picture but knew that was not possible, that this discovery was uniquely Denise's.

'I talked tonight about golden moments,' Denise had reported in June, 'I suppose life shouldn't be a search for gold. The gold should be inside.'

Recalling those words now, Dorine remembered Dublin burgeoning with spring twilight and young men who were allegedly bi-sexual serving behind counters and a certain pain would have ripped from her had her daughter Lara not called and ushered her into a bedroom where the most dominant feature was a reproduction of Van Gogh's apple-blossom.

DESMOND HOGAN

A Poet and an Englishman

1976

WE'LL SHORTLY see the broad beaches of Kerry, he said, smiling, the van ricketing from side to side and Limerick's fields passing, pastures of golden, or near golden, dandelions.

His hair swung flamingly over his face, a wild red gust of hair, and his tinker's face narrowed like a gawky hen's.

'Peader.' She swept her hand through his forehead and he laughed.

'Behold the Golden Vale.'

They got out and looked. Sandra's legs were white after winter, white as goat-skin. A sort of vulnerable white, Peader thought.

Her body was tucked into a copper dress and her hair, red like his, performed little waves upon her shoulders. She looked so handsome. After a winter in Belfast that was strange. One would have thought a winter in Belfast would have changed one, broken down factories and hills, arching with graves.

Yet, in their little house off Springfield Road, they'd hid out, guns going off occasionally, televisions roaring, an odd woman calling.

Peader was working as a tradesman-carpenter-cum-electrician. A strange trade for a tinker, one might have thought. Peader had picked these skills up in London when he ran away from Michael Gillespie, his tutor, in the west of Ireland.

He was seventeen and his hair was more gold than red, and he'd run away from the harbour village in the west of Ireland where he'd been brought up and partly adopted by an English Greek teacher who'd retired to Ireland on the strength of a volume of poems, a hard-bitten picturesque face in the *Times* colour supplement, and an award from the British Arts Council.

There in the west he stayed, making baskets, sometimes taking to the sea in a small boat, writing more poems, winning more awards, giving lectures in Greek to students at Irish colleges.

Peader thought of Michael now, thought of him because somehow the words framed in his head were the sort of words Michael would use.

'A sort of vulnerable white.' Yes, that was the state of Sandra's legs; they were pale and cold. Ready for summer.

'Let's make love,' Peader thought in his head, and he didn't need to say it to Sandra. There were bushes, and leaving their van there on the open road above the Golden Vale, they hid behind bushes, where Sandra could have sworn there was honeysuckle just about to appear, and made love, Peader coming off in her, rising like a child caught in an evil but totally satisfying act.

'Banna Strand.' Peader murmured the name of the beach. Roger Casement had appeared on that beach in a German submarine in 1916 and was arrested and hanged.

'Our first sight of the sea,' Sandra said.

'It's lovely.'

It stretched, naked, cold.

'I'd love a swim,' Sandra thought, thinking of last summer and tossing waves off the Kerry coast.

Peader didn't really notice how pale and beautiful the beach was. He was observing the road, his head full of Michael Gillespie's mythology. 'Roger Casement, a homosexual, arrived on Banna Strand, 1916, was arrested and hanged.' Items of Michael's history lessons returned.

When Peader was twelve, he was adopted by Michael,

brought to his house near the pier and was given a room, alien to him, told by Michael to be calm and often, a little harassed, made his way back to his father's caravan where his father beat his brother Johnny.

The first time Michael referred to Roger Casement as being a homosexual, Peader didn't know what the word meant. He must have been twelve or thirteen when Michael spoke about Casement, and it was probably spring, as spring was a penetrating season in the west of Ireland, lobster pots reeking of tensed, trapped lobster.

When he was seventeen and running away, Peader still knew little about the word, more about a love affair with Michael.

A donkey stood out before them. 'I'll tell him to go away,' Sandra said.

She got out, hugging the donkey's brown skin, kissing his nose, and Peader watched, silenced.

Why was he thinking of Michael now? Why the silences between him and Sandra?

Perhaps because he felt he'd soon see Michael again.

They were going to a festival in Kerry; Peader had given up his job in Belfast, and Sandra and he had bought antiques cheap, and with a van full of them were going to sell them at the festival, which included plays, dancing, lectures, music, drinking, and, most of all, the picking of a festival queen.

Kerry had many festivals, at all times of year, and since Peader's family originally came from Kerry, he'd make his way back there at odd times, like the time in London he threw up his job on a site and went to Dingle for the summer, sleeping in a half-built house, a house abandoned by a Dublin politician who had thoughts of living there when it was fashionable, and when it ceased being fashionable with his mates, he abandoned the place on time for summer and Peader's stay there.

'We'll have a good time, ' Sandra thought. 'We'll have a

good time.' She was smoking a cigarette she'd picked up in a café in Limerick, her head slouched so her hair fell across her face.

'How long is it?'

'Ten miles.'

Her mouth pouted. Her resistance was low; there was a strangeness about Peader. This she knew. Her silence deepened. Cigarette smoking was a token activity.

Maybe it was because of his return to roots Peader was silent. Perhaps he felt sad on coming back to Kerry and the towns of big houses and the verandas of hotels which held rare flowers, because it was warm nearly all the year round in Kerry, a Gulf Stream climate.

'There's a rhododendron,' she shouted.

The first she'd seen that year but Peader wasn't interested and she said to herself 'maybe there's things I don't know.'

She wasn't really a tinker; she'd grown up in Ballyfermot in Dublin. Her father sold junk, broken furniture, broken chairs, broken clocks, and her cousin played a tin-whistle and was married to a Mayo tinker, playing in Germany for a living.

He was famous now, having gone to Berlin, barely knowing how to sing, but by some fluke ending up in a night-spot in a West Berlin bar. Now he had two records and his wife often sang with him, a wild woman with black hair who gave Sandra's family an association with tinker stock.

Sandra had met Peader at a Sinn Fein hop. Neither Sandra nor Peader had any interest in politics, but both had cousins and uncles who supported Sinn Fein and God knows what else, maybe guns and bombing and the blowing up in the North.

Sandra had a Belfast side to her family, her mother's side, and though her mother was silent about Belfast grief, Sandra knew of cousins in the North who wore black berets and dark glasses and accompanied funeral victims, often men who'd died in action. Sandra's main association with the North was tomato ketchup spilling the day she heard her cousin John was dead, a little boy run down by an ambulance which had been screaming away from the debris of a bombing.

She'd seen Peader at the Sinn Fein hop, a boy sitting down, eyes on the groud. A woman with dyed hair sang *'I Left my Heart in San Francisco'* and a girl with a biting Derry accent sang *'Roddy McCorly,'* a Fenian ballad.

Peader asked her to dance - they'd hardly spoken, his hands left an imprint on her back and on ladies' choice she asked him up ; his fingers tightened a little awkwardly about her. The girl from Derry sang *'Four Green Fields,'* as the lights dimmed ; a song about Mother Ireland's grief at the loss of her fourth field, Ulster.

People clapped, and there was a collection for internees in Long Kesh, but Sandra and Peader slipped away ; he slept in her house, on the sofa in the sitting room.

He told her he was just back from England, his first time in four years. He seemed upset, gnome-like, as he was drinking coffee in her home.

She sensed a sorrow, but sorrow was never mentioned between them, not even when they were going to films at the Adelphi or when they eventually married, the wedding taking place at the Church in Stephen's Green, her family outside, black-haired ; his, the remnants from Connemara and Kerry, his brother dressed like Elvis Presley and his cousins and second cousins in a mad array of suits, hair wild on women in prim suits bought at Listowel or Galway for the occasion.

Come winter they went to Belfast, Sandra's Uncle Martin providing Peader with work. Springfield Road, where they lived, ran through a Catholic area, then a Protestant area, again a Catholic area.

Its colour was dark and bloody. Like its history. Catholic boys walked by in blue. Protestant boys walked by in blue. One wouldn't know the difference. Yet they killed one another, violence ran up and down the road, and on in the hills at the top of the road a boy was found crucified one day, a child of ten gagged to a cross by other children of ten, his hands twisted with rope and he half-dead and sobbing.

'We'll leave Belfast,' Sandra said one day, crying over the newspaper. A little girl had been killed down the road by a bomb planted in a transistor set.

'Where do we go ?' Peader brooded on the question.

He came up with an answer, drove back in their van one day loaded with antiques from a bombed out shop. Together they procured more ; 'my father used to buy and sell things at the Ballinasloe fair,' Peader said 'I can take a hint.'

His father and his father's father sold things like grandfather clocks in North Kerry. His father moved to Connemara on marrying Brigid Ward, his mother, and she dying on a wild Connemara night, after he beating her, left two children, John, Peader. Peader was the one taken by the poet ; Peader, now with what Sandra observed as ancestral intelligence, returned to the feel of country things - clocks, paintings of women in white writhing as though in pain - to the purchasing and reselling of these items.

A man waved. Women wandered through the streets, country women, all loaded with bags and with the air of those who'd come from fresh land and flowered gardens. They'd arrived.

'Let's park the van,' said Peader. Sandra had long since forgotten her troubles, but on seeing a young man, a Romany, maybe, with black falling hair, a cravat of red and white and an earring pierced in his right ear, gold, she wondered at their purpose in coming here and felt what she could only decide was fright.

Through the day women with plants walked past their stall, geraniums dancing in pots and women laughing. Business went well.

Craftily, Peader sold his wares, producing more, the

mementoes of County Antrim unionists disappearing here in the Kerry market town.

Relatives of Peader appeared from nowhere; his father's people. Mickey-Joe, Joseph-James, Eoghan-Riam. Men from Kenmare and Killarney.

They'd been to Kerry for their honeymoon, Sandra and Peader, but for the most part Kerry was unknown to Sandra, apart from Peader's accounts of childhood visits here from Connemara, to Dingle and Kenmare, to the wild desolate Ballinskelligs peninsula full of ghost villages, graves, to Dun Caoin and the impending view of the Blaskets and Skellig Michel and the Sleeping Monk, an island which looked like a monk in repose.

'Sandra, my wife.' People shook her hand; grieviously some did it, men who were hurt by lack of sex. He took her hand. They were in a crowded pub and Peader stroked first Sandra's thumb, then took her whole hand and rubbed it.

'You've had too much' said Sandra, but already he was slipping away. She was far from him.

In his mind, Peader still saw Michael Gillespie making his way through the crowd that day. Michael hadn't seen him, but Peader remained strangely frightened, fearful of an encounter.

All the poets and playwrights of Ireland seemed to be here, for it was a festival of writers too, writers reading from their work, writers lecturing.

In the pub now Michael entered. He stood, shocked. His black hair smitten on his forehead. There was no sense of effeteness about him as there used to be. He was all there, brooding, brilliant in middle-age, ageless almost.

'Hello.'

Peader shook his hand – tremorously. So tremorously that he thought of shaking rose bushes in Michael's garden in Connemara when Peader was fourteen or fifteen, frightened by rain, by shaking things.

'Michael, this is my wife, Sandra.'

Michael looked towards her and smiled. He had on a many-coloured teeshirt. 'Your wife.'

Five years since they'd met; it all cascaded now. Peader asked Michael if he wanted a drink but Michael insisted on buying drinks for both of them, Guinness heavily topped with cream.

'To your beautiful wife,' Michael toasted Sandra.

He was here to read his poems he explained, he had a new book out.

'Did you win any more prizes?' Michael was asked.

'Not recently,' Michael replied. But he'd opened a crafts shop in Connemara and anyway he lectured widely now, streaming off to universities in Chicago or in Texas. He had a world-wide following.

'Good to be famous,' Peader said.

'Alone?' Michael questioned.

Sandra was now talking to a boy with a Dublin accent; he had on a cravat and they chatted gaily, obviously having found some acquaintance in common.

'Your wife is lovely.' Remarks loaded, laden with other comment.

Eventually Michael said – sportingly almost.

'How was it?'

'What?'

'London.'

'Alright.'

'Big?'

'At my age, yes.'

'You managed.'

'I was careful.'

Michael looked at him. 'You look O.K.'

Peader remembered the time he was thirteen, Michael minding him, giving him honey in the mornings, eggs fresh, little banquets of eggs with yellow flowing tops.

He remembered the time he was fourteen, by which time Michael had seduced him.

He remembered the white pillow, and in summer the grey morning that would merge into the big room, and afterwards the excitement of sailing a boat or running on the sand.

'Your daddy wouldn't like it!' Michael said one day and Peader thought back to winter and the roadside caravan and his hairy father frying mutton chops that smelt like rabbits dead and rotting.

'You're more handsome than ever.'

'Am I?'

'Tough!'

'Married.'

'You said.'

'I can't say it too much. She'got a gorgeous smile.'

'What have you been doing?'

'Working, writing, lecturing. For two years I lived with an American student from Carolina, a Spanish-American girl.'

'Black haired?'

'Yes.'

'I thought you preferred them blond.'

'Who?'

'People.'

'Peader, you've become harsh.'

Harsh. The winters were often harsh in Connemara; when Peader was fifteen it snowed, and he and Michael freed a fox from a trap near a farm-yard. Peader's hair was quite blond then and rode his head like a heavy shield against the elements.

'This won't last forever,' Michael said one day, weeping.

Peader had emptied a bowl of chestnuts into the gutter at Hallow'een. In a temper, often Peader could be brazen, and perhaps it was this brazenness which drove him to run away.

It was after he'd had an affair with a girl from Clifden, cut through her thighs in a barn near the sea; in a corduroy suit with his trousers down he found woman nearer to satisfaction than man.

He ran away to London, a city of many women, and found no one there interested in him.

No one beyond the odd foreman on a building site, and a man from Kerry who gave him rudimentary training in carpentry and in skills of tradesmanship.

'Are you going to see the festival queen crowned?' Michael asked.

'Yes' – Peader nudged Sandra, 'Will we go to see the festival queen crowned?'

Sandra turned to him. 'Yes. Here's John from Dublin.'

The Dublin boy shook hands with them. They made a party, trailing off.

'Is that the man that brought you up?' Sandra nudged Peader.

'Yes.' His reply was drowned by the crowd, noise, mingling, bunting shaking in the bustling avenues, old women crying raucously, and the young holding one another.

They made their way to a square where the queen was just being crowned, a woman who looked like Marilyn Monroe, her smile big and awkward. Cheers rose about them and fights broke out.

Peader felt himself stirring with an old passion; how many times in bed with Sandra had he longed again to be fondled by male hands and the points of adolescence, his knees, his genitals, to be fondled in the old way.

Instead of having a mother, he'd had Michael. Instead of adolescent tears and rashness, there'd been an even flow, card games, winkle-picking, mountain climbs, a spiral of strange fulfilment.

As the crowd jostled, Peader felt Michael's nervous hand on his shoulder.

'Is your wife having a child?'

'Not yet.'

'Someday?'

'Seed is a strange thing,' Michael said; his words nearly drowned. 'The seed that seems lost but is devoured by an artist's vision, an artist's uncertainty, the uncertainty of reaching to people, the feeling of trying and failing and trying again and loving someone – anyone.'

'Me?'

'Yes – you were the one.'

A balloon went up. It slipped into the air, red, against a rather retiring-looking moon. The fireworks went off, splattered against the sky.

'Like a monstrance at Mass,' Peader thought, remembering childhood and the times his father would take him to Mass in Clifden, the priest turning with a golden, sun-like, object to his congregation and the people bowing like slaves.

Peader virtually hadn't been to Mass since he was seven – except the odd ceremony - like his wedding.

'Let's go somewhere,' Michael said.

'Peader, I've missed you, I've missed your arms and your body. I've waited for you. You can see poems I've written about you and read at Oxford and Cambridge.'

'Sandra,' Peader was going to call out her but she was lost in the crowd with the boy from Dublin.

At three o'clock that morning Sandra made her way back to the tent she and Peader had erected earlier that day. How would she tell Peader? It had been so strange meeting John, a boy from Ballyfermot she'd dated at fifteen. He'd turned into a buxom motor-bike hippie; his pink shirt had drooped open that evening revealing a strongly tanned chest.

'We're all gypsies,' John had said. 'We people from Ballyfermot.'

Ballyfermot, a working class suburb of Dublin.

She'd lost Peader and the man he was talking to in a crowd, a rather strange enigmatic Englishman, and found herself adrift with John.

They'd found their way to a pub situated beside a tin-caravan where fish and chips were being served, and there in the pub had hot whiskeys and recalled going to James Bond films in the Savoy together before John's motor-bike vocation and Sandra's wedding. John had found money in his travels; he'd lived with an old rich Italian lady near Trieste.

'Festivals bring strange people together,' Sandra had said, getting drunker and drunker, leaning on John's leather jacket.

The tent was forgotten and Peader and the rather strange Englishman who had his arms about Peader, the man Peader had often referred to in rather sharp, chipped sentences. She'd ended up lying on John's stomach.

'Let's go to the mountains,' John had said.

'No, to the sea.' Her order was relieved by her mounting the bike and making to the sea. Waves surged in and she ran beside them and John recounted more and more of his experiences in Europe, a night in Nice with a millionaire's daughter, striding by the Mediterranean on the sea-walk below the city with a bottle of champagne.

'Let's make love,' John hugged her.

She relapsed into his arms and lay with him on the sand, but didn't stir to embrace him further, knowing that her faithfulness wasn't to John and the affairs of adolescence, but to Peader and his toughness.

Making her way back to the tent, she thought of Peader and the difference between her and him, a difference she hadn't realized until that night, meeting John again; she'd realized and wondered at the fields of her childhood, fields on the outskirts of Dublin where tinker caravans were often en-camped and which snow brushed in winter, fields grabbed by Dublin's ever-expanding suburbs. Peader had come from a different world, a world of nature continued, ever-present, ever-flowing.

He came from the sea and the west, a world of fury.

There'd been different laws there, different accidents, a savagery of robins dying in winter snow and scarecrows looking like the faces of the people, faces starved for want of love.

Coming towards the tent she heard voices within, male voices. A thought struck her that Peader was within with the Englishman whom he'd been talking to earlier in the evening. It had been a strange, packed way they'd been talking; Peader's clipped sentences returned to Sandra. 'The day Michael and I walked to the sea,' 'the day Michael and I went sailing,' 'the day Michael and I collected blackberries.'

Sandra stopped and listened outside the tent. There was a low moan of pain and Sandra began shaking.

It wasn't cold, but she was sure now of Peader's past; she knew him to be a traitor. He came from a world of lies.

'Peader,' she pulled back the drape of the tent and inside she saw Peader, arm in arm with a young boy she'd never seen before.

She began running, but there was a sudden clench, Peader stopped her.

He was naked and wet. He took her forehead and he took her face.

He kissed her throat and her neck and his tongue dabbed in her mouth. And she fell before him into the cold, dirt-laden, path.

His big and eager face loomed before her. 'It's alright, Sandra,' he said.

'I had to do it and I couldn't hide it from you. There's things to be done and said in life; you must go back, sometimes.'

She'd never know how Michael Gillespie had tried to seduce Peader that night, she'd never know how Peader had repulsed him and walked away, drunk through the crowd.

She'd never know how Peader had picked up a young boy from Cahirciveen who'd been drunkenly urinating and made love to him in the tent, kissed his naked pimples as Michael Gillespie had kissed his years before.

She'd never know, but when she woke in the morning between Peader and a young boy, she knew more about life's passion than she'd ever known before. She rose and put on a long skirt and looked at the morning, fresh, blue-laden, as she'd never seen it before.

Neil Jordan was born in Sligo, Ireland, in 1950, and came to Dublin as a child. A graduate of University College, Dublin, he holds a degree in English and history. He has been writing since the age of sixteen: poetry, plays, and fiction. His first collection, 'Night In Tunisia And Other Stories,' was published in 1976 (Irish Writers' Cooperative), and he was awarded an Arts Council Bursary that same year. He is currently working on a novel, and has completed a television play for the B.B.C. At one time or another he has been a teacher, construction worker, and wine cellar assistant. He is married, with one child.

NEIL JORDAN

A Bus, A Bridge, A Beach

1975

MR. OZARK thought it was the girl he had been following but when she got on the bus and he followed and seated himself and stared at her from over the backs of four rows of seats he realised that it was as much the street around the girl that attracted him as the girl herself. He saw that the girl in the bus was something more and less than the girl in the street. He didn't even attempt to imagine what the girl was on her own, without the street or the bus. In the street there had been the grey suits of men, the hips and arms of women, there had been movement, smoke and sunlight. In the bus there was smoke and sunlight and mostly women and repose.

He was on the lower deck and the cream-coloured walls rose around him and curved sharply into a low, cream-coloured roof. And the curves ran down the bus like a house in a dream until they were stopped by the flat wall that sealed off the driver's cabin. Mr. Ozark heard a voice inside him saying LOOK, a biblical voice with the same authoritative timbre as the sign saying 40 PASSENGERS LOWER SALOON. And so he looked. He looked at the driver's window, he looked at the green blind behind him, he looked at the ad for pork stuck across it. He looked at the girl, framed by the bus, by the glare of light on one side of her coming through the window, by the large fat lady on the other. The fat lady was clutching a grocery-bag with sweating hands and framing them both was the curve of the wall and the lightly-curved roof. He could see the girl full-on and he looked at her as if each detail was part of a graceful sentence, a line he had to know by heart. And then the bus began to move and all the patterns changed as they lurched, turning down Abbey Street. He remembered her on the street moving through the static shadows and looked at her now sitting, passed-over by the quick shadows. Her eyes were fixed on the window but they didn't seem to see the street outside. The window was bright, it glimmered and flashed with the passing houses. The way she looked at it, it seemed to hold a mute, poignant, desperate message for her, perhaps the message she held for him. He kept his head straight as he stared, his back rigid, so his white collar dug into the white flesh of his neck. She had her neck stretched long, like a bird, and her face tilted sideways.

He looked at her features and saw to his surprise that they were a little ugly, a teenage girl's, where nothing seems shaped to fit the rest. She was holding a towel and he remembered how the sight of the towel had made him sweat in his office suit and his sweating and maybe the towel had made him smell the beach again the way he smelled it as a child, a smell of sweat and salt and wet sand. He had followed her, and the smell he hadn't even known he remembered. He had cut out of his mind the Kildare Street office he should have returned to, he had begun to follow and after the first few steps had known he couldn't reverse them and so he had kept walking, filled with a deep, childlike sense of something impending, the fruit of disobedience, though to whom or to what he couldn't have said. And now he didn't even have to walk to carry her, they were both carried, an even space of four seats always between them. He sat watching her, thinking that if the balance of events had been a little different he wouldn't be on this bus now; thinking that if perhaps he hadn't glanced twice at the towel or hadn't seen her boatlike platform shoes, massive under her thin ankles, he would be now among the files of the Department of Agriculture and Fisheries, where he belonged. But he didn't know which of these perhapses was the right one, he felt that all of them, being relegated into a past that didn't happen, were equally impossible. And because of this he felt that his sitting here, staring at the girl with the thin face was as inevitable as the direction in which the bus was travelling. And his eyes took in everything, as if staring round a room he couldn't leave, he had never been so agonisingly conscious.

Of the girl in particular. Her features piece by piece were ugly but led like steps, each one of them, to a perfection that he had never seen before. Or experienced before, since he felt vaguely that someone other than him would have seen her just as a girl, an undernourished girl. And even then his vision of her was impaired. There were two young women immediately in front of him, both with frizzed-out heads of red hair and he had to look through hair, thin rainbows of it, to see her face, thin and drawn at the chin and thrown forward at the cheekbones. Her nose seemed to be going forward too, but in a different, more random sort of way. Her eyes were bulging and black, and they were the smallest, most forward points of her face, since her hair was drawn back tightly across her skull, knotted with a rubber band. It looked oily, clinging, unclean. He couldn't properly distinguish the colour of her eyes, he could only see the black pupil and a transparency, through which she stared at the off-white of the North Star Hotel and the red of Spring Garden Street. There could have been a world there, infinitely more desirable than this one.

He bit into the skin round the nail of his thumb. He had given up smoking years ago and still retained this nervous release from it. And so while his nails were neat and curved, the flesh around them was gnawed, welted. His eyes moved from the girl to the fat woman beside her and then to the ad stuck to the window behind her, half hidden by her fat woman's blonde, melancholy hair. It was for a brand of sausages he had never heard of. It showed a pig with a top-hat and a silver-topped cane performing a grinning dance, its left hand stretched out in negro-minstrel fashion towards a string of flesh-pink sausages. The paper was crinkled and the colours were faded and to him it looked as if the sausage firm had folded years ago, the brand was extinct, only remembered by a handful of posters on city buses. And this thought gave him a familiar feeling, a sense of ending, of having ended, and a wonder at the incongruous way buses moved, people walked, at the way ads still glittered with their strident colours when in fact there was nothing left to buy.

He placed his hands on the metal ridge of the seat in front of him and pushed against it, as if in feeling the pressure of his back against his own seat he was reminding himself that his body was there. The day was hot now, he felt suddenly, gladly uncomfortable, sweat dampening the nape of his neck, running down each armpit. He looked round the bus, round the cool dirt cream of the walls and the blinding light of the windows, at the freely-sweating cotton-clad mass it held and realised he was the only one wearing a suit. It was plain blue terylene, he wore it like a mask, behind it he was liquid, faceless, observant. He watched the sweating bus, his eyes caught the girl again and he stared at her with glazed, released, rancid eyes.

She was dressed cooly for the hot day in a faded orange blouse thing. The material was cheap and the skin at her neck and breast was covered in pimples. He felt somehow that the pimples and the cheapness of the material went together. The blouse was gathered, run-through with elastic all the way down to her waist. He imagined her breasts to be diminutive, adolescent, they hardly bulged at all through the puckered orange cloth. He imagined her staring in a shop window, hesitantly admiring her own reflection. He could see from the way she bit her lower lip that she liked to imitate the pouts of glitter stars. But though normally this would have drawn up a hornet's nest of reaction in him, today he found it beautiful, today he could accept every facet of her, and her lower lip was even more beautiful for its assumed pose of some assumed idol in some colour magazine. He saw her raise her finger and pull her lower lip downwards and he saw how the garish lipstick red on the outside gave way to flesh purple on the inside. And he loved her too for that haphazard application of lipstick, he wondered what store in Henry Street she had bought it in and he became amazed once more at his sudden and private acceptance of this girl he didn't know, he thought of the green walls and tomblike corridors of Kildare Street and of the possibility even now of turning back. He had never before spent a Wednesday on a bus, heading for a beach. But then he had never before followed a girl in an orange blouse, he had never stared so agonisingly. And his life seemed a mundane sleep to him, a useless sidetrack, since nothing in it had prepared him for the mundane shock of this moment. He almost wept for so much time lost, so many hours spent that were not this hour. He felt on the edge of a dream, a dream that was real but that had slept in him till now and was waking now to take over his reality. Its edges rubbed him like a cat's fur.

He felt a jolt and knew that the bus had stopped. He saw the people with the towels getting up and moving and sat till the bus was empty, knowing that she would be the last to go and that he could follow her. He heard the cry of gulls.

He stood watching her and the handful of others walking towards the wooden bridge. He stood there till the bus drew off, watching them being joined by others, all heading for the bridge and the beach beyond it. There was a line of gulls above, flying towards the sea from the city dump. He followed the crowd from a distance, like a straggling gull in a line. He kept sight of her orange blouse, of her bobbing clumsy platform walk.

The bridge was a bottleneck, it suddenly narrowed and

sucked in the crowd, he found himself jostled by elbows, following at the same pace the rapid tread of feet. He had seen holiday crowds before, enough to be critical of their vacant restlessness, but this crowd seemed larger, more pressing than any he could have imagined. The narrow sides of the wooden bridge packed them close together, each of them dressed to meet the sea in their own way, walking towards some point that from their walk, seemed to be in the distance, but from their expression, seemed to be just in front of their eyes. He wondered would what they were walking towards accept him in his terylene suit. He thought of the sea and the sea's horizon, how it always retreats, no matter how near you seem to have got. He decided there would be room for his suit there too. He even felt mildly superior, different in a crowd like this, each of them demonstrating some pertinent gaiety in their gestures. He felt his eyes on the thin back of the orange-clad girl marked him off as almost blessed. He sounded the tough weathered planks of the bridge with his shoes and knew they were leading him somewhere purposeful. He marvelled at the way they had stayed tough, hard and waterproof all these years to allow him to traverse them on this Wednesday, after the thin girl. He noticed some new planks among them, white and resinsmelling and he saw that their edges and hard contours were only beginning to be softened by the tread of feet. He thought of time and renewal and leaned for a moment on the rail and saw the posts that held the bridge falling to the water, doubled by their perfect reflections, echoing back in a series of diminishing vertical lines towards the road. Then he looked up and saw the host of moving backs and realised with horror that he couldn't distinguish the orange blouse. He felt something catching his chest and began to push his way forward through the massed crowd. Then he saw her again, her back, her blouse and he relaxed, amazed at the feeling it brought him of sweetness, of physical relief. She was half-loping, half-skipping to the end of the bridge now, onto the granite walk. Her head was raised towards something he couldn't see. He pictured the beach. He walked faster, surged ahead till he could see her dress for the first time, navy and plain in the fashion of shop-girls. He saw her clearly from behind, the back of her head with her hair drawn back and tied in a knot at the base of her crown, the orange blouse pulled tight with the strands elastic round her thin back. He knew its skin would be like the skin round her cheekbones, thin and stark, with maybe the ribs showing. Then he walked faster, he drew up nearer so that he could have bent forward and touched her hair with his lips. He watched her as she walked, gripping the towel with one arm, gripping a silver-wrapped packet which he hadn't noticed before with the other. He gathered it contained her lunch. He was made almost delirious by the thought that she was totally unconscious of him. It made him drunk with a feeling of almost total power, a feeling heightened by the faint odour of dandruff and vinegar from her hair. He imagined her eating chips and then running her vinegar-wet fingers over her crown. He felt he had the power of life and death in his hands, in his walk, in her unawareness. Then the granite walk ended and they all spilled out onto the strand. He watched her and them, made suddenly tiny by the wide white beach.

In the dream he had entered his office, he had looked at the walls, painted a government green, he had looked at his desk and it was the same, clean except for a paperweight and a sheaf of white paper and an unused glass ashtray kept for colleagues who might smoke. And he had turned and seen the rest of the room, not the same, the walls were plastic, curving inwards, there was a woman bent over the second desk, performing a slow heavy movement with her hands, then a quick light movement. He had walked closer, close enough to see that she was kneading dough, squeezing it with her fingers, then flattening it with her hands, slowly, till it made a thin

cake, then flicking it to one side. And he watched these movements, slow and ponderous, then rapid and light, the flick
always deft and graceful. He had stood watching till the pushing of her fingers became something orgiasic, till the pile of
cakes grew, till she looked up and flicked her hair to one side
with the same flick and smiled. Then he had made for the
door and gone down the tomblike corridor where the files
were kept, running his fingers down the spine of each volume,
looking for the incongruous volume which would explain
her. His breathing was laboured and echoing as he chose one
at random, brushed off the dust, opened it. It was a com-
missioned report on inland fisheries and he searched through
the chapters on the resistance of salmon, trout and perch to
slurry pollutants, searching for the line or something beyond
the line that would explain her...

He filled his day with events, he explained to a colleague
once, and each event gave rise to several more events and so
on, in an infinite series. He would make one phone-call that
would elicit two replies and each of these two replies would
elicit one more phone-call and each of these would present a
small knot that needed unravelling, the unravelling of which
created sufficient new knots for its own justification. And in
the moments between he would create elaborate, meaning-
less conceits in which men ran over hurdles in a field towards
an open space and other men busied themselves erecting
hurdles in the open space for the running men to leap. The
time between events, he explained to a colleague, is a kind of
no-time, preparing for the next event and remembering the
last. He would think of a rosary with no terminal beads, over
which the fingers flickered constantly, searching for a start, an
end, suspecting there was neither.

His memory of his mother's death was not of a tiny figure
among blankets, coughing into toilet rolls, but of a photo-
graphic plate a doctor held to him with dark spaces between
the ribs and lighter curves for the ribs themselves, a smoke-

grey, delicate mist, spreading from the centre, fan-wise. The
following day he had given up smoking and taken to biting
the skin round the tips of his fingers, leaving the nails themselves curved and clean.

He would fall asleep during the Saturday talk programme
and wake up, not knowing how many hours later, to stare at
the empty, perfect-blue screen, to listen to the noiseless
whine and to wonder at the white dot in the centre which
seemed not so much a dot as the only absence in the otherwise
perfect, pervasive blue.

The beach fell away from the road and made a gentle
white curve into the distance. Nothing, not even the figures
dotted everywhere marred the gentleness, the whiteness. He
found it easy to follow her, easy to lose himself. He followed
her across the beach, up the dunes, where she undressed in
the clumps of sharp grass, where he leant against a wooden
hut and watched. A lifeguard came out, with broad sidelocks
and a muscular back, walked past him towards the strand, a
megaphone on a cord swinging from his neck. He saw the girl
slipping her blue dress from her and he saw that the orange
blouse was part of a swimsuit, puckered with elastic from the
waist up. He saw her thin thighs, which he had already
imagined from her neck and shoulders. He saw her walking
towards the strand, much smaller now without her platform
shoes, treading the same track as the lifeguard. When she
reached the sea and walked in, he began to take off his suit at
the sea's edge. He left his clothes in a pile there and walked in,
his white shorts clinging to his hips. She stopped when the
water reached her waist but he waded past her and began to
swim, a small distance out from her. Then he turned on his
back and floated, looking first at the blue sky above him, then
at the sea which was not quite as blue, then at the line where
the sea and the sky met. This line was thin, hardly a line, an
absence. He heard the crackle of a megaphone from the

strand. Someone is drowning, he thought. He turned his head, still floating, and saw the waist of her orange swimsuit above the water. Then he began to flip himself, to roll over in the water. It was a trick he had learned as a child and each time he rolled the horizon swung to meet him and then the sky and the girl in the orange appeared before the water met him again and eventually the girl, the sky and the water were all merged in the tumult of his rolling.

NEIL JORDAN

The Old-Fashioned Lift

1974

THE INNER doors are made of trellised bars of iron. There are two of them, one sliding to each side. The outer door is one pleated plane of steel. It crumples to open, like a folded piece of paper. There is a crash and rattle of metal when the lift stops. Another when the doors open.

It is in the basement of the shop – the wine cellar. And while the upper floors and much of the cellar itself have been modernised, the lift remains, as a monument to the days of coin-shuttles and dumb waiters. And being so old, it functions badly. It won't move at all unless both doors on both floors (for it only serves two – the basement and the ground) are shut tight. Sometimes even the call-button doesn't work. And sometimes it jams in the limbo between ground and basement; where time stops; all else dissolves but the black cuboid sheath.

Thus the sign inside it, in spattered red paint: Please Close Both Doors. And thus the pummelled aspect of the small white button. For when it jams whoever is below will pound on this button viciously and vainly. Once inside, the wires that suspend the lift can be seen through the grid-iron roof. Thick steel ropes, covered in wads of machine-grease. They click oilily and softly as the lift ascends in the black square chute. And at the top this chute is a neat, perfect square of light.

Reg heads for this square of light and retreats from it. Thus his life, a perpetual vacillation between fixed points; points which over the years, deep inside him, have assumed mythical, gargantuan, dimensions. Bunyan's cosmology was never so complete. But with this significant difference; whenever Reg rises, he inexorably must fall. For he carries trollies full of wine and liquor casks to the ground-floor restaurant, and after an interval (during which he wheels them along the street to the restaurants's side door, the lift being clumsily positioned, leading to the street, not the shop) he descends with the same casks, empty now, still balanced on the trolley. Going down he sees the floor-level through the trellised bars, rising to the level of his own feet. Going up he sees the floor above falling gradually to meet him, an enlarging rectangle of light. If he squints his eyes looking upwards, the light spills out from its hard-edged border in trembling technicoloured rays; like a Hollywood sunset, or a vision of the Lamb. But if he looks straight ahead, as he most often does, he sees the chute wall, smoothly black.

Reg is small and irredeemably bent. The stooping he must do to lift so many liquor cartons has caused this. His arms have grown tough and sinewy by the same process. His hands are red and roughened, but delicate somewhere underneath the palm-welt, and looking at them one could imagine him in other circumstances, with another life history, as a delicate, somewhat dandyish old man. Without the sweat-stiff blue polo-neck of course, and the dust-coat. It is grey in colour, struck through with black flecks of a light, felty material and stained down the front to a faded rose hue, from countless wine-spillages. His eyes are like new-formed embryos; webs of centrifugal blood-red lines, leading to a hard, black alive pupil. Here, an onlooker is conscious, the life is; those living, throbbing knots. The mole dwells here that burrows to the light, that meeting it is instantly blinded.

For the most part the eyes are bleared, a little eccentric, a little caricaturish. When an order comes down from the wine-shop they will regard the bringer with a look of assumed doggedness, stupidity. The redness will enlarge and the bringer will react with a: 'come on Reg, up off your arse, then.' But when they approach the lift those hard, black knots will tighten, come alive. Fearing, perhaps the limbo of the black chute.

He spends much of his time away from the chute. Deep in the cellar's interior, slowly and expertly stacking new consignments of bottles in their bins. There is every conceivable variety here and Reg is their arbitrator. Like a medium between the exotic foreign world of wines and liquors and the mundane world of the shop floor. But his mediumship is far from perfect. He gets them second-hand. But once there, they are his preserve. He translates them with a rough expediency. Pouilly Fuissé becoming Pooley Fweezy, Beaune becoming Bown.

He stretches for required bottles with an upheld, quivering hand. He answers the occasional phone-calls in curt monosyllables. He spends lunch-time in the buyer's office, adjacent, sampling glasses from various bottles. By two o'clock he is generally a little drunk. At six he goes to the lift slowly, opens the pleated metal door, steps in and ascends, heading for home. Home he is free of it. But some nights, because of a surfeit of work, or out of some peculiar whim of his own, he spends the night sleeping in the cellar watching its now silent folded joints, gleaming in whatever miraculous light creeps in from the upper floors.

One morning when Reg came down the lift from the street he found a girl in the cellar. Outside there had been a soft drizzle and he was brushing the wet surface of his coat when he noticed her; down from the lift, leaning on the workbench, her light brown hair covering both her cheeks. He stood still for a moment, baffled and a little shocked. Only one other woman ever came here; ever stood against the bench with that much familiarity; Mrs. Ainscott, the cleaner. A plump working woman to whom Reg said, 'Allright Mrs. Ainscott,' to which she replied in the affirmative tone,

'Allright, Reg.' And she generally had finished before the first quarter-hour.

'What?' said Reg loudly, several questions implied. She turned a small elf-like face towards him.

'Oh hello. Is this where I'm meant to be?'

'What,' said Reg again, 'What do you mean?'

'I'm the cleaner, ain't I? Show me what I'm meant to clean.'

'You ain't the cleaner.' And she didn't look it, with her blue smock and her white collared blouse. More like one of those secretaries on the top floor.

'Yes I am the cleaner.' A high indignant tone.

'Don't kid with me.'

'Wot's that then,' she answered, taking a fresh white brush from behind her on the bench. And Reg baulked at this. He couldn't deny it, anymore than he could the stacked bottles or the empty crates.

'Wot's happened to Mrs. Ainscott then?'

'How am I meant to know? Look, you're meant to show me what to clean, aren't you? Well show me.'

'Oh do what you bloody well want.' he grunted. Then, seeing this had no effect: 'Sweep the bloody floor then. As quick as you can. Then get out.'

But she didn't do it quickly. She walked round clattering her dustpan. She bent down to sweep up harmless scraps, her thin buttocks jutting through the blue smock. And Reg stood and watched with his reddish eyes, the black occasionally sparking to the fore. He couldn't work with her there. Everything would be wrong, working with her there. Better wait till she went.

And she didn't go. She began to chatter. After this, she told him, she had to do the ground floor. What was the quickest way up there? Out that door, Reg lied, keeping his back to the lift. Reg took in her face. Its prettiness angering him the more. Her hazel eyes, twinkling brightly when she laughed, her smallboned profile, delicate as a bird's skull, her thick-lipped, saucy mouth.

It was when he heard her questions that he got suspicious.

'Was there a French boy down here yesterday?' she asked, 'a French boy with dark hair and brown eyes?'

'What French boy,' said Reg, 'no French boy down here.'

'Met him up in personnel. Luvley, he was.' She followed this with a peal of laughter.

Reg's eyes narrowed. He said in a low whisper:

'You're not the cleaning woman. You're someone else, ain't you?'

'What do you mean someone else?'

'Someone else, ain't you? Where's Mrs. Ainscott, tell me that!' He saw she couldn't and walked off, as if confirmed in his suspicions. He began stacking bottles, one ear cocked to listen for her exit.

But even after she had left, things weren't the same. His hands shooks while stacking the Piat de Beaujolais and he broke one bottle. He cursed the manager of the provisions department over a mix-up in a calling-order. And at lunch-time the wine tasted sour in his mouth. At six he travelled upwards in the lift looking stonily, morosely, ahead of him.

And the next morning she was there again. Clattering, saucy, still asking after the French boy. 'Wot French boy,' said Reg, and turned to stacking, near the lift end.

On the third day he decided to accept. To accept her brush, to accept the fact of her presence. He stacking, while she swept.

And soon she learns to call him Reg. He calls her Joan. A brief monosyllabic nomenclature, as if she were somehow, a more active, resistant brand of wine than most. But recognition, nevertheless.

Occasionally he glances up from the back of the cellar and sees her bending over a dust-heap, pan in one hand, brush in the other. And instead of blue muslin stretched taut he im-

agines the curve of tender white skin; two shapely pale buttocks with a smattering of hair and long slim downgrowing
legs. It is a minor miracle and one that he finds he can repeat
at will. At first it surprises him and frightens him, but he finds
that if he separates the face and the bright eyes from the limbs
before him it causes him no undue emotional upset.

After each exercise of this double-sight of his he travels
upwards in the lift's oil-glistening black shaft, balancing a
trolley full of wine casks. When he reaches the top he stands
still a moment, basking in the light that filters through the
double doors.

Soon by dint of his double-sight he knows each detail of her
body intimately. She has a mole, he surmises, on the underneath of her left breast. The breasts themselves are small.

From her neck to her breast is a sheer white drop. From her
breast to her thighs another sheer, smooth white drop. He
compares this with the black sheerness of the lift-shaft.

Round her genitals she is almost hairless. The only hair
being on the inside of both legs, near the buttocks. Those
parts of her legs that rub together as she walks.

He finds these sessions more and more engrossing. And
exhausting. So time and again he returns to the lift. Standing
in the light of the ground floor, slowly expelling the taste of
bitterness – like the bitterness resulting from the digestion of
too much over-ripe fruit – from his mouth.

She always sweeps a certain area and then stops. It is as if
there is an imaginary line drawn which she cannot pass.
Around the door, around the work-bench and in the passage
between where the unopened champagne cartons are piled
and the wine bins. For the rest of the cellar, comprising of bin
upon bin of firmly stacked wine-bottles, is Reg's preserve.
During the first few days she made attempts to cover the
whole cellar. Reg, however, constantly barred her passage,
saying repeatedly:

'Mind how you go, Lady, mind how you go.'

She divined his meaning after several repetitions of this. Now, while she sweeps, Reg, in implicit recognition of her function, goes round the bins with an empty carton shovelling in the waste with one hand. So there is this bond between them.

Yet she never takes the lift. She always enters and leaves by the shop door.

And when Reg watches her it is at times as if he is watching an exotic, untouchable bird moving in it's own forbidden lair. And because the line between them is of such finality his fascinated voyeurism is often heightened. Being untouchable, she possesses a strange allure. And she is untouchable because she is base, for women in his mind have always been inexorably associated with the baser functions. So she becomes a maze of fascinating contradictions for him, being both base and exotic, representing pinnacle and nadir all at once. And it is Reg who sustains these contradictions.

One day she straightened herself and turned around to catch him watching. 'Ooo, you dirty old man you. Getting an eyeful, are you?'

And she pulled down her dress smartly, but not without a sense of pleasurable flirtation. Reg turned away, however, muttering to himself so that she could hardly hear him.

'Old bint. What would I want to look at you for. Old bint.'

On another morning, when Reg had to walk past her to get some bottles as she passed, he brushed against her, stooping in the passage. There was the sound, silvery, of nylon brushing off sturdy corduroy. And she rose up with her eyes alight and her lips pursed into a playful kiss. Reg pushed on, like a man trying to avoid a beggar in the street, his outstretched hand quivering. And when he returned from the wine-bins, his arms full of wine-samples, he found her sitting at the bench in tears.

'You hate me, don't you,' she cried. 'Why? What did I ever do to you? What would I want to do to an old man like you?'

And Reg, instead of saying, 'I don't hate you, girl,' instead of feeling for her pliant cheek, the wetness of her tears, with his calloused hand, hovered round the passage mumbling, 'Mind how you go, girl, mind how you go.' And returned to his hand-held carton, to his watching her bend sinuously, like a slow-padding leopard.

And who can tell what led to this, what history caused this restrained rigid hand. The humped hard-skin on the palms, the years spent stacking bottles, lifting till the back curved finally and stuck like a bough stunted, malformed by the impenetrable presence of a nearby brick wall. What days spent walking home through the wall-like streets, what nights between the four walls of a bachelor room till the mind at last assumes its walls, ulcerous, encroaching walls, only the eyes, ultimately, the black, needlepoint pupils left to seek their escape.

What let her weep, and allowed her parade in his gaze then, as before. He always looking, grasping her, rivetting her hugely, archetypally in his senses.

For she is becoming confused in his mind with the lift now. Is assuming the same, gargantuan importance. With the lift, there is the terror of limbo, of being stuck between floors. With her, there is the terror of contact.

He dreams of the lift falling, plummeting like a stone. He wakes screaming.

And one day it happens. He is below in the cellar. He has pressed for the lift, but someone is delaying it. He presses the button again, then pounds on it. The purple veins that cover the bridge of his nose and his cheeks like lichen begin to spread, until his whole face is inflamed. He is late with the restaurant trolley, tilting it backwards and forwards in his impatience. When the lift comes, he opens both doors quickly with his back to them and drags the trolley in. Inside, he closes both doors. Only then does he see her. Standing with her hand at the button-panel, her mouth open in a kind of scared amusement. What are you doing here, he is about to ask, but she anticipates him.

'I'm late, Reg. Have to go up again. Forgot somewhat.'

She moves to press the required button. But he grips her hand. 'You get out,' he says indignantly. 'Come on, you get out.'

His hand on hers is as depersonalised as a vice. She feels it and shivers. But she knows him, doesn't yet grow angry.

'Get off,' she says half-playfully, 'an old man like you.'

This confuses and angers Reg more. 'Out,' he says, 'out,' trying to push her towards the door.

This only makes her more adamant. She squirms past him. 'I work here too, don't I?' she says, and presses the button.

The lift purrs and clicks. And Reg, realising the momentousness of what she has done shouts, 'what did I tell you?' and presses the down button. The lift stops. And Reg's thrumming fingers on the buttons cannot start it again. His face pales as he turns to her, saying in a whisper, 'Now look what you've done.' He doesn't hear her protests or denials. Neither does he look towards the light at the chutes's top. All he sees is the sheer black wall behind the trellised bars. And turning to her, the sheer whiteness of her neck under her clutching, indignant hands. Then he lays hands on her. Not violently or sensually, but coldly, as if it was his purpose, on finding himself hers, to molest her. As if all he must do to molest her is move hands in a pre-ordained way. He touches her face, her neck, her breast. She resists weakly at first, and then not at all, both because of the strength of his hands and some outer, imposing force bigger than he and her. It is he who finally undoes himself. He bends forward with shaking body and steady hands to ravish her waist and unbalances the trolley, which is between him and her. It comes crashing down on him, covering him with cold liquor and sharded glass. She is almost regretful to see it happen. He, as he falls, hears a crashing and crashing in his ears, like the rapid opening and closing of lift doors. Then she presses the button, breathing heavily and goes to lift him saying, 'all right, Reg, you'll be all right.' He doesn't answer, though. So she holds him, looking at his head with wide vacant eyes, waiting for the lift to move.

Photo by Ted Mc Carthy

John Montague was born in Brooklyn (N.Y.) in 1929, and grew up in Armagh, Northern Ireland. He has studied in Dublin (M.A., University College, Dublin) and in the United States (Fulbright Scholar, Yale University; M.F.A., University of Iowa). He has lectured in the United States, Ireland, and France, and now teaches poetry at University College, Cork. Best know as a poet, he has written many books of verse; the latest, 'The Great Cloak,' is a collection of love poems. He was elected to the Irish Academy of Letters in 1969, and in 1976 received the Irish-American Cultural Institute Award. The short story 'Death of a Chieftain' gave its name to the internationally famous Irish musical group, The Chieftains.

JOHN MONTAGUE

Death of a Chieftain

1964

Smith and wesson in one hand, machete in the other, his
T-shirt moist with sweat (except where the raft of the sun hat
kept a circle of white about his shoulders), he beat his way
through the jungle around San Antonio. Behind him followed a retinue of *peons*, tangle-haired, liquid-eyed, carrying
the inevitable burden of impedimenta. With their slow pace,
their resigned gestures, they seemed less like human beings
than like a column of ants, winding its way patiently over and
around obstacles.

When they came to a clearing that satisfied him, he declared a halt, calling up his carriers in succession. The first put
down the table he had been hugging across his shoulders,
peering through its front legs for the path ahead. Around the
table were piled various instruments and items of food with,
to top the mound, a bottle of *tequila* and a neat six-pack of
Budweiser beer. With the air of an acolyte bringing a ritual to
its conclusion the last carrier approached, lugging a battered
cane-chair. Bernard Corunna Coote sat down, breathing
heavily.

Food came first. Like a bear let loose in a tuckshop, he ransacked the parcels, tearing the tinfoil or polythene bags open.
Half an hour later, while the natives lay around, somnolent as
stones after their brief meal of *tacos*, he was still fighting his
way through a cold roast chicken, washed down by draughts
of lukewarm beer. Finally, wiping his mouth, he turned to
work.

Compass and sextant, lovingly consulted, pinpointed his

position. Then he erected a triangular instrument, like a theodolite, and took readings, both horizontal and vertical. As though satisfied of where he stood, but not what he stood on, he produced a gleaming spade and began to sink holes around the clearing. From them he took 'samples,' handfuls of red clay and stone, which he heaped on the table, to the height of a child's sandcastle.

By the time he was finished, the whole clearing looked as if it had been attacked by a regiment of moles. From under their conical hats the Indians watched: now it was their turn. Exasperated by their sleepy gaze, he dispatched runners into the forest to bring back further samples. When they returned to lay their spoils before him (curiously shaped fragments of flint, stones faintly resembling arrowheads, stones in which veins of mica flashed) he interrogated them about anything they might have seen, with an optimism that only gradually died into disappointment.

All these details were entered on a large roll-like map of the district. At the top of the chart, in a fair hand, was inscribed the Indian name of the region: *Coatlicue,* the land of the God of Death. At the bottom was the owner's name: *Bernard Corunna Coote, His Property.* In between, from the central axis of San Antonio, the ever increasing lines of his excursions radiated outwards, like a spider's web.

If the centre of the spider's web was San Antonio, the centre of San Antonio, as far as Bernard Corunna Coote was concerned, was the Hotel Darien. It stood on a promontory overlooking the town, a great bathtub of a building whose peeling façade was only partly disguised by a fringe of palm trees. The disparity between its size and the adobe hovels gathered around its base would have been shocking, were it not for its enormously dilapidated appearance, like a rogue mosque. From whatever angle one approached, its grey dome was the first thing to become visible; a landmark to the market-going Indian, slumped on his burro, a surprise to the traveller, who felt as though he were arriving at Penn Station or St. Pancras.

The history of the Hotel Darien combined mercantile greed with the despairing quality of romance. In the 1890s, after the failure of the de Lesseps Panama project, a group of Liverpool and New York businessmen (already linked by the golden chain of considerable shipping profits) had been taken by the idea of cutting a railroad through the jungles of Central America. Such a railway would save ships the dangerous journey round Cape Horn : cargo could be shipped across the isthmus in a day. The tiny fishing villages at either end would become great ports, where the goods of half a continent were transferred from boat to rail and vice-versa. And so the Hotel Darien came into existence, a luxury hotel where top-hatted businessmen could relax, gazing proprietorially out onto the Pacific.

And then, in 1902, while the first cowcatcher was pushing its way through the jungle, news came that the United States had taken over the Panama Canal project. The Hotel Darien did not die immediately : one does not destroy a white elephant if it has been sufficiently expensive to construct. The railway came in due course and though the opening was less spectacular than planned (the President's speech was drowned in a tropical thunderstorm) there was a little light traffic, especially tourists attracted by the idea of travelling through savage country, with a stout pane of glass between them and the alligators. But gradually it degenerated into a jungle local, staggering from village to village, its opulent carriages white with bird-droppings.

Business picked up slightly in the 1920s with the planning of the Pan-American Highway. But even that passed about fifty miles away and only occasional parties deviated to San Antonio, drawn by the legend of the railway or by the few excavated archaeological remains in the area. Gradually the

Hotel Darien sank to what seemed its place in the scheme of
things, a remote limbo for remittance men, unwanted third
sons, minor criminals, all those whose need for solitude was
greater than their fear of boredom. And strays from nowhere
that anyone had ever heard of, like Bernard Corunna Coote.

Bernard Corunna Coote came to San Antonio in the late
summer of 1950, part of a guided tour from Boston. He
looked out of place from the beginning, a large man, sweating it out in baggy flannels and tweed coat, with, perched
incongruously on his forehead (like a snowcap on a tropical
peak), the remains of a cricketer's cap. He stank of drink and
had the edgy motions of someone who had not slept for days :
black circles were packed under his eyes.

His companions skirted him as they descended from the
bus. Only one person showed any interest in his arrival : from
his niche under a pillar on the shady side of the square, Hautmoc, the town drunkard, opened an opportunistic eye. When
the American matrons chattered off, armed with cameras, in
search of the colourful town market, Hautmoc moved in. He
found Bernard Corunna Coote sitting on the terrace of the
town café, drinking *tequila.*

'Señor?' he said, with sweeping politeness, 'may I join
you ?'

When the main party of SUNLITE TOURS returned, Hautmoc
and his companion were still deep in conversation. Originally
spotted as a soft touch, something in the uneasy bulk of his
victim had moved Hautmoc, who was busily explaining to
him his favourite subject : the ethnological basis of American
civilization. His mahogany face, mystical with drink, leaned
towards the white man.

'But in the mountains, beyond the Spaniards' reach, the
poor people remained,' he oracled. 'They—we—I am still a
pure race.'

Coote did not speak, but his eyes flickered interest.

'Spaniards, bah ! a decadent syphilitic race from a dead

continent. Mexicans, bah ! a spawn of half-breeds. The true Indian...'

The SUNLITE TOURS bus was loading in the square. As the negro courier looked over, sounding his klaxon, his passenger ordered another *tequila*.

'You were saying ?' he asked.

'The true Indian, *los hombres de la sierra,* are the aristocrats of this hemisphere, the purest people in the world.'

The courier came towards them, touching his hand to his yellow SUNLITE cap.

'Mr. Coote, we're leaving now, sir.'

Bernard Corunna Coote turned up a watery, but firm, eye. 'I have just discovered the purest people in the western world,' he said in Spanish. 'In such circumstances, one does not leave. *Yo me quedo aqui.*'

As the bus roared from the square, a surprised line of New England matrons saw their late travelling companion and an unknown Indian, their two heads together, roaring with laughter. Between them, like a third party, stood the new bottle of *tequila.*

'In the old days,' said Hautmoc, with a meaningful gesture towards the bus, 'we would have sacrificed *them.* A land must be irrigated with blood !'

And thus Bernard Corunna Coote became one of the permanent guests of the Hotel Darien, and as much a feature of the town in his own way as Hautmoc. Daily he padded down to the square for a morning drink, and to collect his mail. According to the postmaster, a quiet student of these matters, most of the letters bore a king's head and came from Inglaterra. But there was also a newspaper bearing the ugliest stamps he had ever seen, a pale hand clutching a phallic sword, and surrounded by what looked like (but was not, as he found when he consulted the dictionary) Old German script. It was all mildly puzzling, and he took the unusual step of being polite to Hautmoc when he next met him, hinting at a free drink if information was forthcoming. But as everyone had long ago agreed, the latter was a cracked vessel, returning little or no sound, except his pet theories about race and human sacrifice.

'I don't know,' he said, screwing his eyes like an animal dragged into the light. *'Es muy difícil.* He says he is from the oldest civilization in Europe, as old as the Indian. But it is not English.'

To the rest of the town he was *el Señor Doctor,* the brooding figure whose place at the café table no one ever took, even on market days. The schoolboy cap had given way to a wide-brimmed sun hat, the tweed coat had disappeared, he wore floppy cotton drawers, and rope-soled sandals instead of Oxfords, but they could still recognize a learned man when they saw one. Even if mad : catching those large, watery eyes upon them the women in the market-place drew their *rebozos* over their heads and made a gesture of expiation as they bent to rufflle among their baskets of fruit and pottery.

II

The people in a position to know most about *el Señor Doctor* were those who appeared to care least : the three other permanent guests of the Hotel Darien. The oldest was not really a guest, being the hotel manager, but he had so little work to do (and that little he tended to leave to the servants) that only rarely were his companions reminded of their business relationship with him. A cadaverous Iowan, called Mitchell Witchbourne, his bony features had the asceticism of a Grant Wood painting : one looked behind him, expecting to see a clapboard barn and silo. This impression of weathered starkness was increased by his high-pitched voice. Night and day it creaked, like a weathervane, sending out stories, jokes, hints of what looked like hope and communication, but gradually took on the shrillness of signals of distress. At forty he had been manager of a chain of Mid-Western hotels, from Chicago to Colorado : what had brought him, ten years later, to a decaying seaport on the Pacific coast ?

No one knew either what had brought Jean Tarrou, the neatly moustached little Frenchman who spoke English with a slurred brokenness which grew more charming each year. A devotee of *la culture physique,* his room was full of mechanical contraptions upon which he practised nightly. (An American matron, hearing the sounds from the adjoining room, had burst indignantly in to find him squatting in black tights on the carpet, one hand held high, the other pointing sideways, a human semaphore. His legs were caught up in pulleys, towards the ceiling, at an angle of forty-five degrees.) Now and again he dropped hints of a distinguished past, a *licence ès-lettres* from the Sorbonne, consular service in the West Indies, but the trail came to an abrupt end with the last war. He had served under Vichy, but did not detest de Gaulle, a paradox which indicated that his troubles were as much private as political. In any case, like most French people, he did not discuss matters with people outside his family circle, even when, as in San Antonio, they were either far away, or non-existent.

The person about whom most was known was Carlos Turbida, who was still young enough to derive satisfaction from the idea of being a black sheep. The son of a wealthy Mexican fish merchant, his father had retired him from the capital after his third paternity suit (it was not the behaviour he objected to, but the carelessness). Officially, he was in charge of the south-west section of the family fishing fleet, and, once a week, he roared away in his Porsche to the nearby harbour. Tarrou had seen him there, the distinctive olive-green machine parked among the fishing nets while a bored captain pretended to listen, as he strutted up and down the quay. He even cultivated a sailor's walk, but the effect was not so much athletic as sexual : he rolled his hips as though carrying a gun. But generally he lay in bed, eating sweets, reading movie magazines, and dreaming of Acapulco : the perfect portrait of the Latin-American *cicisbeo*.

Their main interest in Coote was mathematical : he made the necessary fourth for most card games, poker, bridge, gin rummy. To endure the silence of a place like San Antonio habit was indispensable. Five evenings a week they played, grouped around a table on the veranda, while the tropical night grew heavy outside, and the Indian waiter came, bringing a lamp, and fresh drinks. At first they played for *pesos,* but then, disdaining the effort of tossing coins on the baize, they turned to counters, using match-sticks as chips. As the sums involved mounted—from tens they progressed to hundreds and sometimes thousands—even that kind of tally became impossible. So each time the soberest of them (it was usually Tarrou) kept a record. Though their skills were roughly equal, it was necessary, to keep an edge on the game, to believe in some apocalyptic day of reckoning : in the meantime, there was the drug of ritual contest, with memory floating to the surface as the hands were occupied.

'I remember once,' said Turbida, 'driving from Monterey to Mexico City. You know the road ?' He raised two fingers to indicate a bid.

'Up, up, up,' said Witchbourne, sawing an imaginary steering wheel. 'Then, down, down, down.' He clutched his stomach.

'I spent the night in a little hotel, high up in the Sierra Madre. In the corridor, outside my room, I see the, how you say, chambermaid. She has long black hair, down her back, a pure Huastecan Indian. As she pass, I take hold of it.'

'I pass,' said Tarrou, and poised his pencil over the white slip of paper at his side.

'Let me go, she cries, let me go. There were tears in her eyes. I say, I let you go, if you come back to stay. That night, I sleep with her six times. She cries again when I leave in the morning. What can you do with silly girls like that?'

'You can only eat them,' said Tarrou, pleasantly.

'I'll see you,' said Coote, hunching his shoulders across the table towards Turbida. The latter laid down his hand calmly: in the heart of his palm two dark queens lay, without embarrassment, beside two smiling red knaves.

'Damn,' said Coote.

There was silence while Tarrou shuffled the cards, laying them (with that pedantic precision he brought to every action) in a neat semi-circle before each man. If Turbida's stories were mainly sexual, his were more frightening, tasteful vignettes of people and places which only gradually revealed, under their smooth surface, an underlying terror.

'It is on that route, if I remember rightly,' he said, 'that the natives bring one glasses of freshly crushed orange juice. The bus stops by the groves just at midnight and the whole air is full of the smell of oranges.'

Both Witchbourne and Coote reached simultaneously for more whiskey.

'But it is not quite as gracious a custom as on the route to Vera Cruz,' he continued. 'There is a little station there, just before the railway descends from the mountains, where the women come, selling camellias laid out in hollow canes, like little coffins. It is only then that one notices that most of the women are crippled: one has no fingers, another no nose, a third a stump instead of a leg.'

'Heredo-syphilis,' said Witchbourne gruffly, 'the Spanish pox. These mountain villages, no water, no medical services, intermarriage: never get rid of it.' His moustaches were bright with whiskey.

'I bid you a hundred pesos.'

'I raise you fifty,' said Turbida excitedly.

As Coote threw in his hand, Tarrou leaned forward, delicately poised as a cat. 'I will raise you both fifty,' he stated.

After a further flurry of bids, the others faltered, throwing in their hands. While Tarrou recorded his victory, Witchbourne swept up the cards for the next deal, glancing swiftly at the Frenchman's as he did so : three fours.

Of Witchbourne's conversation there was little to be said : the past for him was a devastated territory, a no-man's-land, through which he wandered, picking up fragments. Hardly anything he said could be added to anything else, the only recurrent factor being his practice of ending the evening by telling a joke. And his favourite was the story of *The Vicar and his Ass*. When he began, everyone tensed, assuming stares of interest, like executives on a board meeting.

'There was a parish in the mountains where the people had a long way to go to church. So they all went on their asses, and to pass the time, they played games, the boys pinching the girls' asses and the girls' asses biting the boys' asses. Then they tethered all the asses at the church door. One day during the revolution, a bomb fell in the graveyard. In the confusion, everyone jumped through the windows, the boys falling on the girls' asses, the girls on the boys' asses. As to the vicar, he missed his ass altogether and fell in the bomb hole. Which goes to show...' Witchbourne paused dramatically. Tarrou and Turbida seemed frozen, their features pale with insulted sensibility. Only Coote, who was hearing the story for the first time, gave the necessary prompt.

'What ?' he asked.

'That the Vicar did not know his ass from a hole in the ground,' said Mitchell Witchbourne with satisfaction. As the waves of unease spread around the table, he gathered up the cards and rose to his feet. 'Beddy bye,' he said softly, disappearing off into the darkness. The others looked at each other with the expression of people who did not know what to think, and did not dare ask.

It was in this atmosphere—a harmony woven of night

sounds : the warm darkness beyond the veranda, the tinkle of ice-cubes, the rise and fall of voices—that Bernard Corunna Coote felt impelled to his first confession. Having drunk more than usual one night, he announced, with sudden confidential exactness :

'I am a renegade Protestant !'

There was silence for a moment. Then Witchbourne, who was dealing, flicked an eyebrow upwards. 'Ach so,' he said, in guttural parody.

'We have few Protestants in Central America, as a such,' said Turbida. 'They do not seem to go with the climate.'

'You do not understand,' said Coote, beating the table with his glass. 'I am a renegade Ulster Protestant.'

'I have heard of the Huguenots,' said Tarrou politely. 'And, of course, the Hussites and Lutherans. But I do not know of your sect : is it interesting, perhaps, like the Catharists or Boggomils—Eros rather than Agape ?'

'You still do not understand,' said Coote fiercely. 'I am a renegade Ulster Presbyterian ; an Orangeman !'

'Ah, a regional form of Calvinism,' said Tarrou sweetly. 'We have had that too : the Jansenists of Port-Royal. But you should not let it worry you.' He studied his cards carefully before raising three fingers. 'Catholics, Protestants, Communists, *nous sommes tous des assassins.*'

A silence fell, heavy as the night outside. It was broken by the sound of Bernard Corunna Coote weeping : one tear fell, with a distinct plop, into his whiskey glass. His large head, flabby with drink, runnelled with tears, looked like a flayed vegetable marrow. The game continued.

After this rash beginning, Bernard Corunna Coote learned to offer his confidences with the same casualness as he played his cards. And though (unlike the latter) they lay without immediate comment, he knew that they were being picked up, one by one, gestures towards a portrait. Assembled, they made what Tarrou once smilingly called

LE PETIT TESTAMENT DE BERNARD CORUNNA COOTE.

Bernard Corunna Coote came from a distinguished Ulster family, descendants of Captain William Coote, who was rewarded for his skilful butchery in the Cromwellian campaign with a large grant of Papish land. Industrious in peace as war, he was the founder and first Provost of Lagan-bridge : an equestrian statue (brave, beetle-browed, a minor hammer of the Lord) still stands in the town square, on the site of an old palace of the O'Neills.

The family seat, however, was at Castlecoote, overlooking the river. At first, little more than a four-square grey farm-house or 'Bawn' (fortified to prevent the sorties of dispos-sessed Catholic neighbours), it was redesigned by John Nash in 1755. As they watched the new building rise—the door-ways flanked with fluted Doric columns, the noble rooms with elliptical designs on the ceilings, the terraces dimin-ishing to the river—something seemed to happen to the family features.('You could see it in the portraits,' said Ber-nard Corunna Coote, 'they felt easier, less predatory, more secure.')

In this handsome Georgian building, generations of Cootes grew up, the eldest managing the estate (and generally the county as well, being Grand Master of the Orange Lodge), the younger going into colonial service, the daugh-ters marrying other Plantation squires, their equals in land and religion. The only break in this pattern came when war broke out : then, as one man, they rushed to the side of the King. Hardheaded, with the bravery of the Irish, but more sense, they made magnificent soldiers, especially when com-manding a regiment of their own tenants. A Coote had led the crucial charge at Corunna, a Coote had been aide-de-camp to Wellington, a Coote had led the Ulster division on the Somme. Whenever the Empire was in danger, a Coote would take command, looking at the battlefield as though it were a few hundred acres of his own land and say, with a brisk return to the vernacular : 'WULL DRIVE THIM THRU THERE !'

To this tradition, compounded of the sword and the ploughshare, was born a son, Bernard Corunna Coote, a sore disappointment. His whole career seemed a demonstration of the principle of cultural reversion, i.e. the invasion of the conqueror by the culture of the conquered. His childhood was spent listening to old Ma Finnegan, the Catholic tenant in the lodge gate : she taught him the Rosary in Irish and the tests for entering the Fianna. His holidays from public school were spent roaming the hills in a kilt, with an Irish wolfhound at his heels. From these walks sprang his vocation : in his third year at Oxford he announced that he was going to be an archaeologist, an expert on the horned cairns of the Carling-ford culture, the burial places of the chieftains of Uladh.

He was on a field trip, deciphering standing stones in the Highlands of Donegal, when war broke out in September 1939. Bernard Corunna Coote could no longer resist family tradition : he joined as a volunteer in the North Irish Horse and fought in both the African and Sicilian campaigns. But though he acquitted himself well (whatever else, he was no coward) the contrast between how he regarded himself and what was happening to him became too much to bear. The first his parents heard of it was when he was reported as refusing a decoration 'on the grounds that he did not recognize the present King of England.' A campaign for the use of Gaelic in Irish regiments also brought comment, coinciding as it did with the preparations for D-Day. In-valided out of the army in 1944, he did not (at his father's request) return to Castlecoote. After rattling around Dublin for a few years, he disappeared to America.

III

From these confidences, delivered so haltingly, heard so

calmly, Bernard Corunna Coote received the peculiar form of
comfort which was the secret of the Hotel Darien. His companions spoke rarely of what he had said (the only direct
comment was Tarrou's puzzled remark that he did not see
what all this had to do with religion), but he knew that it had
been heard, and if not understood, accepted. He became one
of the members of an invisible club, an enclosed order whose
purpose was not so much contemplative as protective:
behind these walls they seemed to say, you are safe, all things
are equal, you may live as you like. He no longer sought
Hautmoc (Lord High Muck, Witchbourne scornfully called
him, his name being that of the last Aztec chieftain who tried
to propitiate Cortez by a mass sacrifice) for long conferences,
though the latter still watched him from behind the pillars of
the arcade as he went to collect his letters. Apart from that
morning stroll he had been assimilated into the world of the
hotel.

It was some months, however, before he was introduced to
the second ritual of the permanent residents: the visit to the
town whorehouse. Every Sunday afternoon, led by Mitchell
Witchbourne, dazzlingly spruce in white ducks and
embroidered shirt, they made their way to an old colonial
house at the other end of the town. This spacious building
belonged to Dona Anna, a mestizo matron whom Witchbourne – remembering some comic strip of his youth about
an orphan girl – had nicknamed Obsidian Annie. She was not
really an orphan, but the widow of an officer who had taken
the wrong side in the Revolution. Finding herself stranded in
San Antonio, she had applied her strong, practical nature to
developing the primitive prostitution system of the area – the
famous 'double-baths' of festival days – into a regular business. Under her care she had usually about half a dozen
young ladies, ranging from sixteen to thirty, with the dusky,
almost negroid beauty of the women of the peninsula.

Events at the Casa Anna always followed a definite order,

the decorum of Sunday blending with the lady's desire to do her best for her most monied visitors. First, the girls appeared, wearing their holiday best, long flounced skirts, embroidered lace *huipls* or bodices, and heavy ear-rings made out of United States gold pieces. Dona Anna, of course, being one of *los correctos*, the people of good standing, wore a stiff dress of dark Spanish silk, to distinguish herself from such peasant finery. They all had a social drink together while the men made their choice (there was usually a new recruit to spice routine). Then they withdrew to their rooms where, beside each *palias* stood the inevitable bottle of *tequila*. Through the long afternoon everyone loved or drank or watched through the windows the boys shinning the banana trees, like insects on a grass blade. Now and again there was a satisfying plop! as one fell into the undergrowth.

It seemed a good life.

As darkness gathered, everyone came together again for the evening meal. This took place in the dining hall, the largest room in the house, with fortress-like doors opening onto the patio. At the head of the table presided Obsidian Annie, a clapper by her side to summon the two white-coated Indian house boys. As the food piled higher (local delicacies like turtle eggs, or iguana roe, with purple yams and pa-payas), a kind of wild gaiety seized them, the girls shrieking as the men pinched them through their thin finery. Even Obsid-ian Annie relaxed her vigilant decorum, growing nostalgic as she drank from the stone jar of fresh *pulque* at her side. Tears trickled down her thick make-up as she remembered the days when she had been a young girl, the great days before the Revolution: Obsidian Annie was not a democrat.

'And on Sunday we all rode together in Chapultepec Park. Oh, you should have seen us, the girls sitting side-saddle, wearing black hats and skirts, and lovely Spanish leather boots. And the men, with their silver buttons and braids, in the *charro* style, as handsome as Cortez!'

It seemed a more than good life.

The delay in introducing Bernard Corunna Coote to the second ritual of the Hotel Darien was cautionary: they feared that the same forces which had pushed him to total confession would push him further, and that they would lose a hard-won recruit. But they need not have worried; he and Dona Anna got on together like a house on fire. Previously it had been Tarrou who had been her favourite, as coming closest to her aristocratic ideal; in moments of tenderness she called him Maximilian, remembering the blond prince who had tried to bring French civilization to her country.

But between a suave member of the middle-class and something approaching the real thing, there was no question. In clasping Bernard Corunna Coote to her firmly corseted bosom, she clasped her own youth, a bloated version of the *caballeros* who had escorted her through Chapultepec Park. And from her flatteringly warm embrace (a blend of fustian and volcano), he seemed to extract a maternal solace.

True, he had bouts of restlessness, but they were the 'thick head' of the novice, rather than real rebellion. Whenever he sulked, refusing to come to the banquets by which she set such store, she went to fetch him. Soon they were drinking and singing together, he calling her 'his favourite g-e-l' and teaching her the songs of the Continental Irish brigade:

> On Ramillies field we were forced to yield
> Before the clash of Clare's Dragoons...

The only person upset by this arrangement was Tarrou, who discovered in himself vestiges of a jealousy he thought extinct. But having given up life *as a such* (to use Turbida's phrase), why quarrel with one aspect of it? His wit grew more strained, his stories more silkily sadistic, but his ill-humour did not seem to theaten the equilibrium of their communal life. Not, at least, until the night of the May Festival, several months later.

For the members of the Hotel Darien, the May Festival was the major trial of the year, the one day when the town broke in on their consciousness with an usurping rattle and roar. A famous local patriot had said that a Revolution should be as gay as a Carnival: in his memory, San Antonio made its carnivals as violent as revolutions. From the tolling of the cathedral bell in the morning, through the Blessing of the Goats at midday, to the processions in the evening and the Grand Ball at night, it was one long orgy of noise. Indians in gaudy finery pressed through the street, shouting and waving banners: by nightfall most of them were roaring drunk, challenging all comers with their machetes.

In previous years the inhabitants of the hotel had made halfhearted attempts to join in the fun. But they could never relax or feel at home, the locals parting before them as they came to the wooden beer canteens in the square, their connoisseur's interest in the blind flute-player turned to mockery as they passed, the local matrons parting with relief from their embrace in the dance tent, with its flaring gasoline lamps. As they left, they heard the music spring up again, its vitality underlining their isolation:

> Woman is an apple
> Ripe upon a tree –
> He who least expects it
> May have her beauty free;
> And I pray to San Antonio
> *That it may be me!*

Their object became to close it out of their consciousness. They could not go to Dona Anna's establishment because (cupidity getting the better of her aristocratic inclinations) it was full of drunken Indians. Neither could they relax in the garden or on the terrace: the noise was too great. So they remained indoors, with all the windows and doors locked. But the heat became so intense that they felt they were drowning. Even under the fans there was no relief, the metal wings only stirring the thick air.

By nightfall they had gathered in the hotel lounge, in the vague hope of playing their customary game. But they were all drunk, with that peculiar restlessness, that draining of energy which a day's drinking brings. Together with a nervous irritation: Tarrou's voice was razor-sharp with menace.

'Shall we begin now?' he asked, for the third time.

No one spoke. There was a burst of cheering that made the windows rattle. A firework rose in the air, broke and fell, illuminating the room with a sudden glow.

'Shall we begin?' said Tarrou again, rapping the deck of cards on the table.

Still no one spoke. Another firework climbed within the square of the window. Coote watched it moodily: he felt isolated from the others and had the impression he was missing something.

'I see you are impressed by our peasant customs,' said Tarrou, with acidity.

'They do make a lot of noise,' Witchbourne interposed.

'You are not the only one, or course,' continued Tarrou. 'Dona Anna also likes them, although she pretends not to. It is easier to impress peasants.'

'But not so much noise as some city people do,' said Turbida, hastily joining Witchbourne's rescue operations. 'There is a rough night-club behind the Reforma where as soon as the girls appear everyone shouts —' He expired in giggling lecherousness.

But Tarrou was not to be cheated of his prey so easily.

'The noisiest night-club I ever knew was on the borders of

the Goutte d'Or district in Paris : you know, the Arab quarter. There was a fat Algerian tout there, a sort of barker. Now that I come to think of it, he resembled our friend there...' He gestured towards Coote, who shifted slightly in his chair. Like an animal entering a slaughterhouse, sensing the glint of steel hooks, he was becoming aware of the menace directed towards him.

'The only time there was silence in that club was during the act involving the Siamese twins. Some day I must tell you about that.'

'Some day,' said Witchbourne, gruffly.

'I remember —' said Turbida again.

'But the Siamese twins, though an interesting act, lacked the simplicity, the imaginative daring of the barker's own speciality. I have told you he was an Arab. He wore a long flowing burnous : at first I thought it was for local colour. But at the end of the evening, he removed it, slowly. It was only then that one realized — *on le soupçonne toujours d'ailleurs, avec les types gros comme ça...*'

'What ?' asked Turbida, in spite of himself.

'That he was a woman. A big, fat, ugly, aged woman.'

There was silence. Mitchell Witchbourne's face was white. But it was Coote who spoke, finally, dragging his great bulk up.

'You go too far,' he said raspingly. 'Even in hell there are limits.'

IV

Happiness is a balance, precariously maintained : to achieve even its semblance requires training. While the others, with instincts geared to survival, swept the incident aside, Bernard Corunna Coote clearly could not. For days he avoided the hotel and news drifted back that he had been seen drinking with Hautmoc. After a while, he began coming again to meals, but when Witchbourne ostentatiously produced the card table he disappeared, and they heard him crunching down the avenue towards the town. He did not even return to the Casa Anna, though Obsidian Annie inquired after him, saying that she had seen him (again with Hautmoc) at the local café. It was agreed that Tarrou should speak to him. One night, as Coote was ploughing back through the darkness, the slim Frenchman presented himself at the door, his cold eyes taking – but not returning – the latter's surprised glare.

'We do not see you now,' he said pleasantly.

Coote did not answer, all his efforts absorbed in the task of breathing. But he moved forward as though to brush past Tarrou.

'Why do you not join us in the evenings any more?'

Coote stopped. 'You know why.'

'*Mais, mon ami,*' Tarrou spread his hands, gently. 'These things are unimportant. *Dans l'ivresse, comme dans l'amour, il faut tout pardonner.*'

Coote looked at him for a long time, and his eyes seemed to clear in the hallway light. Then he moved forward again, resolutely.

'May mwah, jenny pooh pah,' he said, in his harsh Ulster accent.

For his former companions of the Hotel Darien, however, no answer was final. They did not begin to despair of him even when he disappeared on his first 'expedition.' It looked so harmless, a large man with a morning-after face and stubble, going off into the jungle by himself, carrying a hammer. And the bag of samples he brought back, examining them for hours on the terrace, were like the coloured beads a child might play with. But when instruments and books began to arrive at the postoffice and the day's wanderings spread into weeks, they began to be alarmed: in the organized quality of these frenzies, they recognized an alien discipline. Swallowing his pride, Witchbourne went out of his way to speak to Hautmoc, and inquired as to their purpose. The latter graciously accepted the drink offered him, but was far from helpful.

'He is looking for something we have both lost,' he said mysteriously.

Smith and Wesson in one hand, machete in the other, his T-shirt moist with sweat (except where the great raft of the sun hat kept a circle of white about his shoulders) he beat his way through the jungle around San Antonio. Behind followed a retinue of peons, tangle-haired, liquid-eyed, carrying the inevitable burden of impedimenta. With their slow pace, their resigned gestures, they seemed less like human beings than like a column of ants, winding its way patiently over and around obstacles.

Even the rainy season did not halt him, physical obstacles being only a drum-call to the military ardours of his ancestry. Coming to a flood-swollen river he would plunge in, his weapons held high above his head : sometimes only the hand and the round circle of the hat could be seen as he sidestroked heavily across. If there was a current he would float with it, until he struck an outcrop. Then, like Excalibur, he broke to the surface and trampled ashore, water dripping from his bulk, as though down the side of a mountain, By the time his followers had crossed (going to a village for the loan of a pirogue, or wading downstream until they found a fording place) he had already blazed a trail into the pelvic rankness of the jungle on the other side.

What the Indians thought of their master—a comic *gringo* if ever there was one—was at first tactfully submerged in the fact that he paid well. Sufficiently well for them to want to humour him when, following some atavistic memory of a Victorian jungle trek, he insisted that they should carry their own packs and leave their burros behind. But as the months passed, something of his anxiety communicated to them : just

as they sped with eagerness on his errands, so they watched
with increasing concern his disappointment as he turned over
the stones they had brought. A man, they knew from their
own lives, could only bear so much misfortune : in Bernard
Corunna Coote's case they felt that some incongruous
struggle was going on, an almost physical rending, as though
a blind man were trying to see, or a cripple to walk.

Sometimes he would stop short in his tracks, as if struck by
a blow from behind. The pale blue eyes would glaze and turn
inwards, the shoulders hunch, until he looked like the oldest
of earth's creatures, some grey mammoth embedded in ice or
rock. And the cry that he gave, low at first, rose till it seemed
beyond human pitch, a trumpeting that tore the heart with its
animal abandon.

It was after one of these outbreaks (dutifully reported by the
servants), that the inhabitants of the Hotel Darien decided
that a last effort should be made to save Bernard Corunna
Coote for themselves. For to their surprise they had
·discovered that they needed him. From selfish exasperation at
the loss of a necessary companion, they had passed to real
concern, and an emotion that only their long habits of reti-
cence refused to recognize as love. It was though their bluff
had been called, and the suffering they had gradually relegated to the background of their own lives had suddenly
reappeared before them, monstrous, dishevelled, wringing
its hands.

But what was to be done ? They had a formal meeting in the
hotel lounge ('the scene of the crime' as Turbida said brightly,
before Tarrou's coldly speculative eye fell upon him) to
discuss the situation. Tarrou's attempt to apologize had
failed. Witchbourne's efforts to elicit information from
Hautmoc had been fruitless. There remained Turbida, the
soiled innocent of the party, whom no one would ever suspect
of any serious motive. Witchbourne's mild eye joined

Tarrou's in resting upon him. Turbida must find out what Bernard Corunna Coote thought he was doing.

The opportunity came a few days later when Coote returned from a long absence in the jungle. He looked more exhausted than ever, with a rough growth of beard and a tear in his trousers which exposed long thin legs. But he did not seem surprised to find Turbida in his room, his expensive shape splayed over a cane chair.

'Good day—— ?' the latter asked, with the upward inflection of the hunting classes.

Bernard Corunna Coote snorted, but did not answer. After depositing a sack in a corner, he dragged off his clothes, and stepped under the shower. Through the yellow curtain Turbida could see his body, a whale under water.

'I have been looking at your books,' shouted Turbida, lifting up a volume, with a large painting of a pyramid on the cover.

Still no answer. The shower sank, a hand groped for a towel : Bernard Corunna Coote emerged, clean, spiky haired, decently clothed in white.

'Interesting chaps, these Aztecs, when you get right down to it,' continued Turbida, turning the pages. 'Place like Monte Alban now, makes you think....'

Coote stopped pummelling himself. 'You have been to Monte Alban ?' he asked incredulously.

'Why, yes,' said Turbida, trying desperately to remember the illustrations Tarrou had shown him, 'and to Mitla too.'

'Did you see the scrollwork at Mitla ? The cruciform chambers ?'

'Yes, yes...' encored Turbida.

'The spiral and lozenge pattern are the same as at Newgrange. It was a characteristic of the race, the delight in abstract pattern. But we were a thousand years before.'

Turbida was about to inquire where Newgrange was when

he saw that Coote was no longer listening to him, his face contorted with fury and anguish.

'Think of it ! When Cortez and his Spaniards came, they found the Maltese cross, and the Indians spoke of strange white men. Certainly it was Brendan——'

'Brendan ?' echoed Turbida.

'Saint Brendan who discovered America. But what about even earlier ? We know that the Celts were a widely dispersed people : traces of them have been found in Sardinia, Galicia, the valley of the Dordogne. We are the secret mother race of Europe. But if——' he halted, as though transfixed by the daring of his thought.

'If,' prompted Turbida.

'We could prove that the Celts not merely discovered but *founded* America ! Think of it—' He brought his face close to that of Turbida, who could smell the furnace blast of cheap spirits.

'Then, for the first time, the two halves of the world would fit together, into one, great, universal Celtic civilization.' He raised his arms high, then let them fall slowly again. 'All I need is a proof.'

'Like what ?' asked Turbida in a hushed voice.

'Oh, there are minor ones. Character for example, Haut-moc says that the original Indians were the purest race in the western hemisphere : we still place a great emphasis on purity. And *physique*; remember the bearded statues of La Venta ?' He tugged his own beard vehemently, to emphasize each word. 'After us, there were no bearded men in South America.'

'But a major proof ?'

Coote seemed to hesitate. It was months since he had spoken to anyone : should he now reveal his hopes to a comparative stranger ? Only the music of international renown could heal several generations of outraged tradition : here, in San Antonio, Bernard Corunna Coote was staging his last fight to restore himself not merely to his family, but to the whole history of human knowledge.

'I told you once of the cairns of Carlingford and the Boyne, the burial places of our early chieftains. From the decorative motifs I deduce a connection between them and the pyramids of the lost civilizations of Central America. But the pyramids, according to Hautmoc, were designed for human sacrifice only, and not for ritual interment. If I could find...'

He hesitated again, drew a deep breath.

'Somewhere, in the most remote areas, probably in the thick of the jungle, there must be traces of those earlier structures upon which Monte Alban, Palenque, Chichén Itzá, were based. If I could find one single passage grave or burial chamber...'

'Like what?' asked Turbida again.

'Like this!' cried Bernard Corunna Coote, seizing and opening a large green volume. 'Look!'

Carlos Turbida was still trembling when he joined the others an hour later.

'But the man is mad,' he cried plaintively.

'The question is irrelevant,' said Witchbourne, with unaccustomed severity. 'Which of us is even half sane?' His gaze swept across his companions, like a searchlight across rocky ground.

'Still, it is strange,' said Tarrou. 'I was sure he was cured. Who would have thought the irrelevant could have such deep roots?'

'But nothing can be done. It is too late...' wailed Turbida again.

'It is never too late,' said Witchbourne sententiously. 'While there's life there's hope. What do you think, Tarrou?'

'I think,' said Tarrou, 'that the time has come for our famous reckoning.' From his pocket he produced a sheaf of white dockets, neatly bound with rubber: he ruffled it under their noses.

'A sum of of money is always useful,' agreed Witchbourne.

'But then, what will you do?' asked Turbida.

Tarrou shrugged. 'We shall see. I will perhaps go and talk to our noble friend, Lord High Muck.'

'But what about?'

'About literature,' smiled Tarrou. 'Where is that book you say Coote gave you?'

V

The rainy season passed. The mouth of the San Antonio River was no longer choked by floating vegetation, and the long dugout canoes could sail directly up to the market place. The mountain paths had dried and the peasants came down to the village in ox-carts, lined with layers of crushed sugarcane. The few meagre crops were to be harvested, maize, sesame seeds, beans. Soon the first tourist bus would turn into the square, to halt for an hour or so before continuing its journey southward.

It was on the anniversary of their first meeting that Hautmoc came to Bernard Corunna Coote with unexpected news. The latter was sitting at his accustomed place on the terrace: he had not been on trek for over a week, and looked more than usually morose, his shoulders slouched over the café table. Behind him hovered the proprietor, fearful not that he would attack anyone (despite his noise, the gross foreigner was surprisingly gentle, not like the common-class of Indians who broke loose with their machetes when drunk) but that he should do himself harm: the day before he had fallen on his way to the lavatory. Now and again, from that seemingly quiescent mound of flesh, a hand would emerge, and grope around the table for the bottle which was poured, with many whistling sighs and groans, in and around his glass.

It was then that Hautmoc appeared on the far side of the square near the post-office. It was hard to miss him because, after several months of unaccustomed prosperity, he had deserted his trampish practices and dressed as befitted a descendant of kings, with an elegant *serape*, slashed in scarlet and black, and a white sombrero. Moreover he was walking briskly, almost running, with an abandon that surprised Bernard Corunna Coote, who had been talking to him the night before. He came directly to the café table, but did not sit down, gazing at his friend and employer with a kind of tranced look:

'Master,' he said solemnly, 'we may have news.'

Bernard Corunna Coote stirred uneasily. 'What do you mean, you may have news?' he grated.

Hautmoc looked over his shoulder, towards the café-owner, indicating that he did not feel free to speak. 'We may have important news,' he repeated.

With an effort, Coote threw out his arm towards the chair opposite him. 'Sit down and have a drink.'

'There is no time,' said Hautmoc, slowly. Then he leaned his head swiftly down towards the other's sunken face, and whispered into his ear: 'We have found what you were looking for.'

Bernard Corunna Coote started. Did Hautmoc know what he was saying? Like the shepherd boy suddenly face to face with the wolf, like the alchemist seeing a yellow liquid condense in his crucible, he gazed at him, slowly believing his eyes.

'Where?' he asked, rising from the table, his face aglow.

The sun was low in the sky on their second day's march when they reached the area indicated by Hautmoc. It lay near the source of the San Antonio River, a region Coote had rarely explored, believing it already well known to the natives. But perhaps he had been wrong to ignore it: after all, river-beds were the traditional centres of civilization. But so high up? For hours they had climbed up the mountainside, through the thick forest of the lower slopes, where springs made the ground soggy and treacherous. Then they crossed a belt of shale and rock, where the river sank to a trickle, and they found animal skeletons bleaching in the sun. Finally, towards evening, they emerged onto a small plateau set, like a shelf, against the steep incline.

A light wind was blowing. Below them, the valley fell away, a matted sea of vegetation, divided by the thin line of the river. There was no sign of a living thing, the smoke from the occasional village or clearing being absorbed in the transparent mist that lay above the trees. At the limit of their view the sun was sinking, like a coal at the heart of a dying fire.

'Is this the place?' said Bernard Corunna Coote, impatiently.

After easing off their packs, the Indians had gathered around him and Hautmoc, as though waiting for an order. The latter did not answer, but remained looking out, in melodramatic serenity.

'Is this the place?' asked Coote again. 'Where is it, or what is it called?'

'It is called Coatlicue,' said Hautmoc seriously. 'It is one of the most ancient of our sacrificial grounds. The people took refuge here during the Conquest. There used to be a temple.'

'But where —' demanded Coote fiercely.

'Behind,' said Hautmoc. Folding his serape around him, an elegant figure in scarlet and black, he turned to lead the way.

In his excitement at the view, Bernard Corunna Coote had not yet had time to look behind. Now, following Hautmoc, he turned. Above them rose a rock face, sheer as a wall, making the area in which they stood seem artificially compact, like an apron stage. The outer edge of the plateau was covered with a hide of tough yellow grass, knotted so close that it made walking difficult. This yielded to a close undergrowth, where lichened boulders lay around like ruins: to Coote's astonishment there was the semblance of a path through it, stained with burro droppings. This led to a clump of well-watered trees: was it the source of the river? Parting the damp oar-shaped leaves, Bernard Corunna Coote saw an open space ahead, a clearing at the entrance of which Hautmoc and his fellow-Indians had gathered to await him.

In the middle of the clearing stood a group of stones. As he drew closer — scattering the natives to right and left like ninepins — he saw that they formed a shape, the unmistakable humped outline of a tumulus. There were two stones on either side, with a closed passage at the far end. There was the great flagstone, resting on the five stones as smoothly as a table top. The whole thing was symmetrical, textbook perfect, even the dark quiet faces grouped around seemed in harmony — except for one thing. As Coote approached, his foot crushed something in the grass. Whoever had hoisted the flagstone had forgotten to remove the pulley rope. It wound imperceptibly down the crevice between the two nearest side stones until, like a snake, its end struck up at the sole of Coote's sandal.

He stood there, looking from the rope to the construction, and back again. Then he followed the rope to its source, under the top stone, and tugged. The stone shifted, audibly. He stepped back and gazed for a long time, until even the Indians – professionals of the steady gaze – felt uneasy. Their leader came over and touched him on the shoulder but Coote did not move.

'Master,' said Hautmoc gently, 'we meant no harm.'

Coote still did not reply, his eye rolling over the same square of space, like an eager student crazed for an answer.

'We would not have known how to build it, but for Señor Tarrou. He taught us. And Señors Witchbourne and Turbida provided the money for the workers.'

Coote looked at him, vaguely. 'But you, why did you do it? You told me you would have nothing to do with them.'

The dark face of the Indian seemed to crease and open, as though reliving a painful decision.

'They' — he pointed to his fellows around — 'did it because they wished to please you. I —' he hesitated.

'Yes?' demanded Coote.

'I did it because — because if the place you are searching does not exist, then it should. Your dream and mine have much in common.'

Coote looked at his companion for a long time. Then a hint of a smile crossed his face.

'Hautmoc,' he said majestically, 'you are even madder than I am.'

But the other was not listening, his eyes resting fondly on the stones before him. 'There is still one thing lacking to prove us both right,' he said sadly. 'Such stones cry out to be used.'

For a long time Coote's expression did not change, as if he had not heard what Hautmoc had said. Then he straightened, his great back cracking, and looked at the Indians around. They returned his gaze with expectant, admiring eyes, as though his countenance reflected the pure bronze light of the dying solar god. Knowledge passed swiftly across his face, a spasm of lightning.

'I understand,' he said gravely.

Slowly, with the dignity of a military ceremony, he removed his large sun hat. His face was a hunk of meat, fiery red, but above it his bald head shone, the whitest thing they had ever seen. He stepped briskly forward, the Indians falling in line behind him. When he came to the passage grave he marched straight in, leaving them to file to one side, where the loose rope dangled.

'Pull,' he ordered, settling himself in the trough of red clay. As he waited for the heavens to fall, his countenance became relaxed and pure, all provincial crudity refined to a patrician elegance, the ripe intensity of a soldier leader born of two great traditions. Softly on fields of history, Ramillies and El Alamein, Cremona and the Somme, the warpipes began to grieve. Closing ranks silent regiments listened, Connaught Rangers and Clare's Dragoons, Dublin and Inniskilling Fusiliers, North Irish Horse and Sarsfield's Brigade. The stone started to creak.

'After all, it is a good way for a chieftain to die,' he thought contentedly.

Photo by Dom McPhee

John Morrow was born in Belfast, Northern Ireland, in 1930, and left school at fourteen to work in a shipyard. He has been in the linen trade, a day labourer in England, and, until recently, in insurance. (He lists his education as 'Public Elementary, Duke of York Bar, and paperback.') He has published humorous short stories, and had contributed short stories, features, children's serials and spoof pantomime to B.B.C. radio. In some of these he sings his own parodies, a reflection of an earlier success as a folk singer and instrumentalist. The Arts Council of Northern Ireland awarded him a Bursary in 1975. He has written one novel, 'The Confessions of Proinsias O'Toole' (Blackstaff Press, 1977). He lives in Belfast with his wife and two sons.

JOHN MORROW

The Humours of Ballyturdeen

1976

'WE'LL HAVE less of that sectarian nonsense, Jeffers, if you don't mind,' said Mr. Sanders, re-aligning the signed photograph of Mr. Bob Cooper ('Alliance – Voice of the Silent Majority') in relation to his immaculate blotter. 'The fact is,' he went on, 'that there are units in Ballyturdeen crying out for repair and until we can arrange a replacement for Baxter –'

'– Who chose the Prison Service sooner than Ballyturdeen,' observed Jeffers firmly, causing Mr. Sanders' hands to ball suddenly into small fists.

Jeffers was sure of his ground; the brawn drain of men to the Prison Service, the Police Reserve and Securicor was one of Sanders' own hobbyhorses at Rotary Club luncheons... 'You know as well as I do, Mr. Sanders,' he said, 'That soldiers get D.S.O.s just for having been in Ballyturdeen. On the T.V. only last week, when the Queen Mum presented colours to the 2nd Flintshires, what do you think was the new battle honour on the battalion flag, below El Alamein and along-side Waterloo –?'

'– I know, Jeffers, I know,' cried Sanders, 'we all watch –'

'– Ballyturdeen,' stated Jeffers, making his point. ' So I'll have triple-time or my cards.'

'Triple!' yelled Sanders, causing his girl Friday in the outer office to hunt out the yellow pills. 'My God, Jeffers, this is blackmail – industrial blackmail! And I shall not have it. Do you hear me, Jeffers? – I shall not have it. I shall not allow myself to be intimidated... People like you are worse than the bombers and gunmen – using the troubled times in our dear land to further your own selfish ends... Industrial bully-boyism! That's what it is... But remember, Jeffers, at the end of the day 'We must love one another or die;' 'No man is an island', Jeffers...'

Jeffers listened patiently. He knew there was no real harm in the man. And the decibel count was rather less nowadays than when he'd joined Spinduo as a boy ten years ago and Sanders had been a leading light in amateur dramatics (the memory of those daily, Bard-laden confrontations still gave him the shudders). Since then he had seen Sanders through Humanism, Moral-Rearmament, the Jehovah's Witnesses, and he'd found that when the quotations began to fly the best attitude was the stonewall. Other men, skilled in W.E.A. dialectics, had shouted Sanders down, confounded him, left him with his Faith (in whatever) tottering – and received their cards and holiday money in the next morning's post. As one long gone agitator had said of him: 'His heart's in the right place – but his head's full of mad dog's shite.'

Ten minutes later, after a performance by Sanders of all but the tail-end of Beethoven's Ninth on bumpaper and comb, Jeffers went through the outer office and said to Girl Friday: 'Triple-time from now, love. That's official.' She, anticipating the frantic bleeping of her dictaphone and hurrying Sanders-wards with yellow pills and water, growled 'Redflagger!'

'Blue knickers,' replied Jeffers, administering a deep re-verse goose with twist and sending Girl Friday, water and pills in three different directions. Sanders bleeped piteously.

But once on the motorway at the end of which, somewhere, lurked Ballyturdeen, Jeffers' spirits sank. Behind him lay the homely, smoking ruin of Belfast; there he knew where he was, or where he shouldn't be, at any given time, in his head a tracery of invisible battle-lines created by polarisation ('git out or brunt out, ya taig/prod basters'); a city of vast pigeon-holes – including a burgeoning ghetto of Chinese waiters around the municipal bath – in which he had become attuned to every nuance of change that spelt danger: the midday stillness that might herald a sudden swarming from sidestreets, like maddened bees from a smoked hive, as some hungerstriker gasped his or her last; the abrupt acceleration of a police land-rover for no apparent reason; the look on the face of a searching paratrooper that told him not to remark pleasantly on the state of the weather or England's position in the World Cup...

But Ballyturdeen?... What did he know of it beyond the three names familiar to every Dervish and Bushman with a transistor tuned to the B.B.C. World Service: 'Kilbraddock's Braes' and 'Turberry's Meadows,' its two Housing Trust kraals, and the notorious 'Cut,' the blood-spattered no-man's-land which separated them and which for three years had vied with Sinai and Penang Province for the attention of the world's camera crews. There, only six months ago, an entire C.B.S. unit had been wiped out in crossfire after failing to come to a suitable financial arrangement with either side. And there too had occurred the terrible massacre of a delegation of CofE liberal vicars (though in mitigation, a case of mistaken identity due to poor visibility and misted gunsights – for one side the profusion of fuming briar pipes had been enough, for the other a brief glimpse of flared houndstooth and one flowered kaftan).

Yet when Jeffers pulled off the motorway an hour later and made a tentative probe into the Ballyturdeen outskirts, all seemed very quiet. He left the van at the barrier which closed off the main street to all traffic (including, hopefully, car-bombers), intending to present his list of calls to the nearest shopkeeper and ask directions. Shutters everywhere – it was whole-day closing. Cursing his luck, Jeffers walked the street both sides, but the only living thing he encountered, a hunch-backed septuagenarian dressed up as a traffic warden, scuttled away up an entry as he approached... The alternative, Jeffers decided reluctantly, was that last resort for anyone wanting to get anywhere in the shortest time possible: the police.

He had passed the barracks on the way in; a fortress, with all but the front wicker gate sandbagged and the entire building caged to the roof in an anti-bomb screen. When he rang the bell on the gate a voice crackled over an intercom from within: 'Who are ye? What d'ye want here?' After he had stated his business there was a hiatus while they conferred and took a long-lens photo, he supposed. Then the voice said, menacingly: 'Stay where ye are. I'm coming out.'

What came out first was the muzzle of a Sterling machine pistol, behind it a grizzled, brick-faced retired farmer in the uniform of the Reserve Force. Jeffers first presented his identification for scrutiny and then his list of calls. The Reservist squinted at the list, whistled, pushed his cap up from his forehead, muttered something rural like 'Boys-a-dear!' and fixed Jeffers with a look of fatherly concern... 'The man that give ye this lot, son, didn't much like ye,' he commented ominously.

'Why's that?'

'I'll tell ye why: two of them's in Kilbraddock's an'three's in Turberry's. That's why.'

'Oh... Well, what's it like in there now? Quiet?' asked Jeffers, wondering if he should turn around, go home, and bugger the triple-time... But if only he could get in and do one job in each area ('Not-at-homing' all the others) Sanders would then have no excuse for welshing on the triple-time — as he knew Sanders would try to do in any case.

'Quiet?... I dunno,' growled the Reservist; 'nobody knows. They could be atein' each other for all anybody knows.'

'Do you — I mean the police — do youse patrol up there?'

'Patrol! Yer jokin'!' the Reservist guffawed at the idea of it.

'The only patrollin' done up there is from an army helicopter on very dark nights. An' I hear tell all it does is hover a fut or two off the groun' long enough for one fella to jump out, shout 'Goal!' an' jump in again!'

An exaggeration, Jeffers knew: that was another branch of his antennae developed over the troubled years; the wilder the tale, he'd always found, the milder the basis of it...
'Well, I think I'll go out and have a look anyway,' he said, folding the list. 'What road do I take?'

'On yer own head be it, son,' sighed the Reservist, turning and pointing the Sterling. 'Keep on the way yer facin'; over the ramps; through the barriers at the army sangers there an' you'll come to the internment camp on yer left; follow the wire to the end, take the first on yer right an' about a hunnerd yards up yer into the Cut... I wouldn't chance the van in it, if I was you — you could wreck the sump in them mine craters. But you can take side lanes into the estates — Kilbraddock's is on yer right, Turberry's is on yer left... Oh aye, an' if ye run across any T.V. men up there that wants an interview, it's ten quid a time, mind. We don't want youse city fellas comin' up an' spoilin' the rate. O.K.?'

'O.K.' said Jeffers, and was turning away when he remembered... 'Oh, constable — you said three in Turberry's and two in Kilbraddock's; but what about these other two here?' He began to unfold the list again, but the Reservist forestalled him: 'Oh aye... Yer alright at that end. It's a private estate — shally bungalows. I live out that way myself,' he said proudly.

Five minutes later Jeffers, heart in mouth, bumped along the Cut and turned off in the direction of Turberry's Meadows. The entrance to the estate was marked by the burnt-out husk of an army scout-car, the insignia of the Life Guards still visible on the turret. It swarmed with squealing youngsters and barking dogs, reminding Jeffers, ironically, of those mobile recruiting exhibitions that tour country towns on market days. He eased the van past without attracting so much as a look, let alone a stone.

Encouraged, he drew up alongside two ladies gossiping over a gate and asked the way to his first call (all the street nameplates and door numbers had been removed). They directed him volubly. One, noting the firm's name on the pocket of his overalls (he had decided to use an unmarked van) said: 'Ma Gilmore'll be glad to see you. Thon oul hurdy-gurdy of hers has been stone dead for months.'

No wonder, the motor housing crammed with old, boiled cabbage secreted there by Ma Gilmore's five greenhating urchins... But before getting round to that diagnosis, having been greeted like the Prodigal by Ma Gilmore, Jeffers had three cups of tea, half-a-dozen Paris buns and a lot of re-assurance...

'– Niver heed a word them shits of Peelers tell you, son,' said Ma Gilmore, a cheerful, chain-smoking goitre victim; 'there's nobody'll lay hand on you this side of the Cut. An' there's no need to tell you to steer well clear of them savages on the other side.' (He'd thought it better not to mention his calls in Kilbraddock's)... 'I'm still sure an' certain that's where my Tommy is,' Ma Gilmore went on bitterly, the saucer eyes that go with her ailment beginning to overflow, 'lyin' stiff as a board with a bullet in him under somebody's garden in Kil-braddock's. My own brother swears he seen him fallin'-down-drunk outside a pub in Scunthorpe, but nothin'll ever convince me he wasn't waylaid by them animals... Ethel thinks the same about her Frank. Isn't that right, Ethel?'

Ethel, seated on a low settee, smiled and nodded and tried to stretch the hem of her skirt another inch towards her crossed knees (only another six to go). Ethel – Mrs. Lavery, twenty-four-year-old mother of two – lived next door and her Frank had flown the coop four months ago. Jeffers ob-served that she had not allowed grief to affect either the bond or the elaborate dressing of her false eyelashes. He also no-

ticed some other outstanding things about Ethel and was wondering if she had a Spinduo machine when Ma Gilmore, as
though reading his mind, said: 'Why don't you get Mr. Jeffers
to have a look at your fridge, Ethel?... It hasn't been de-
frosting properly since Frank went. Isn't that right, Ethel?'
Ethel smiled and nodded... 'There's such a lot goes wanting
when there's no man in the house. Isn't that right, Ethel?'
Ethel giggled and Ma Gilmore, the neighbourly soul, gave
Jeffers a meaningful look...

It was a form of social work in which Jeffers had had a
wealth of experience – the only sort for which a Degree is not
required, only talent... So after digging a bucket or two of
putrid cabbage out of Ma Gilmore's hurdy-gurdy he accompanied Ethel to her house, leaving her two children
happily unravelling Ma Gilmore's surgical stockings – a
favourite treat.

Knowing nothing about fridges anyway, he got down to the
task in hand without delay (pure habit, for the time factor
wasn't as crucial as when working a tight call schedule in the
city). Ethel's reaction from start to finish was in keeping with
her social repartee – 'Oh... Oh?... Ah!!!' – after which he had
a job keeping her awake long enough to get her from the kitchen floor to the sofa.

He left her snoring and returned to Ma Gilmore's, who,
thoughtful soul, had a cup of tea waiting. 'Well, you can't say
we're not full of hospitality in Turberry's Meadows – you
dirty brute!' she cried, punching him playfully... The sudden
thought that Ma Gilmore might be contemplating an agent's
fee in kind caused Jeffers to gulp his tea and bolt for the van.

So far so good, he thought, tooling gingerly around the
craters in the Cut: one call in Kilbraddock's and we're home
free. (Of his other two calls in Turberry's, one tribe had flitted
in the night a week before, Ma Gilmore had told him, taking
with it the bath, the upstairs toilet, every inch of copper
piping in the house and the roof-tiles, and the other lot,

friends of hers, were using the complaint ploy to stretch their
H.P. terms to infinity. Against the first Jeffers wrote 'Derelict
house' and against the second 'Con-artist.')

In every respect save wall graffiti Kilbraddock's Braes was a
mirror of Turberry's Meadows. True, there were no war relics
quite so dramatic as Turberry's scout-car, but a seemingly
haphazard pile of builder's rubble near the entrance to the
estate, Jeffers noted, had no missile in it more than hand-
sized... On the Green a mixed group of teenagers played a
game – a not very nice game – with the rubber baton rounds
the army use for mob control. Some spectators who lounged
beside a stand of Japanese motorbikes wore the remains of
policeman's caps, mutilated to resemble Brando's headgear
in 'The Wild One,' recently revived on T.V. But Jeffers
reached his call unmolested.

His first sentiment on meeting the lady of the house, a Mrs.
McKenna, was heartfelt pity. All the fear and insecurity of the
times seemed personified in that little beak of a face peering at
him round the door-jamb... 'Spinduo service, Missus,' he
announced – and immediately regretted it. The face went all
open-mouth-and-staring-eyeballs   before   disappearing
inside. Jeffers heard her running up the hallway crying, 'Spinduo, Teddy... Oh dear God, Teddy, Spinduo...' and following, he thought to himself that here was the end product of it
all: the bombs, the bullets, the night searches, the whole
gruesome business of near civil war...

At the kitchen door he was confronted by Teddy, the man
of the house – large, toothless, badly in need of a truss,
but still brutal looking about the tattooed forearms. He
held a quivering finger under Jeffers' nose and shouted,
'And about time too! Either you fix that bloody thing in there
or take it to hell outa here or I'll hold you and bloody
Spinduo responsible when they take that bloody woman
away!'

In the kitchen Mrs. McKenna cowered in one corner and

stared at her gleaming Spinduo Combined-Twin-Tub-and-Spin-Dryer in the other.

'What on earth's the matter, Mrs. McKenna?' asked Jeffers, shocked at the state of her – and not a little fearful of the angry bulk of Teddy crowding in behind him.

'You'll get nothin outa her,' bawled Teddy. 'Look at her: skin an' bone, nails ate to the elbow – an' eight weeks ago she cudda flung a full milk bottle twenty-five yards... Till that bloody thing came into the house!'

'But what exactly's wrong?' asked Jeffers, crossing to the machine.

Mrs. McKenna shrieked and fled from the kitchen. Her feet pounded on the stairs and a door slammed overhead.

'There y'are,' said Teddy accusingly; 'that's her for the day. You'd bloody better –'

'– But if you'd only tell me what's the matter,' cried Jeffers, his own nerves beginning to jig in sympathy.

'Tell you!'... Teddy jabbed a fag-pickled finger at the machine. 'No need to tell you anything. Just you pull that bloody switch there an'you'll see what's the bloody matter!'

Jeffers did – and within seconds realized with horror, and some awe, that for the first time in ten years he had drawn that one in ten thousand: a rogue; a 'Dr. Who...'

He had often read about the phenomenon in trade magazines and had heard many tall tales of the havoc wrought on all who came in contact with it, never dreaming that one day he'd be called upon to cope... And it had to be to-day of all days, and in this bloody place, he thought angrily, watching the machine waltz gracefully across the lino towards him...

'What did I tell ye!... What did I tell ye!' screamed Teddy, skipping into the hall and half-closing the door. 'An wait'll you hear it... Wait'll it warms up...'

When it reached the extremity of its lead the machine paused. Clothes and suds swirled in the window of the main tub (after its last performance the McKennas hadn't dared remove the load). Then suddenly it gave vent to the first in a series of huge guttery farts, the red and green lights on its master panel began to flash on and off, and its lead, pirouetting and, eeriest of all, singing... 'Listen to it,' moaned Teddy from the hallway; 'Faith of Our Fathers'... an' there's worse...' Jeffers himself thought it more like a slow version of 'The Battle of Garvagh,' but said nothing.

As though cued by Teddy's voice the machine had begun to gyrate faster, fart louder and sing shriller. Jeffers, fascinated despite himself, noted the curious fact that for all its wild shimmying it never touched anything; it skimmed cupboards, circled the table, birled down the length of the lead and up again, always missing by a hairbreadth as though it had evolved in itself some sort of radar screen...Then, just as music, lights and movement seemed to be mounting to a fused crescendo, everything stopped ('This is it! Wait'll you hear it!' howled Teddy). After a short pause – when, Jeffers was to swear later, the rogue breathed heavily – came the first part of 'it:' the most ear-shattering fart yet. This was followed quickly by a deep but distinct groan 'Ah-h-fu-gg-h..'
for all the world like an expression of sincere relief by a costive docker, as the 'Dr. Who' voided its load of suds onto the lino. The lights went out.

'Did you hear that! Did you hear that!' screeched Teddy, outraged, bounding in to launch a kick at the satiated machine. 'Sure wouldn't that wreck the nerves of any dacent married woman... Now either you tame that baste or get it away to hell outa my sight!'

Jeffers had read and heard enough to know that there was no way of taming it. Indeed, as he now told Teddy, they were all very lucky that it had not yet reached the homicidal stage inevitable in such mutations. He quoted instances of householders, crisped to a turn, being flung through windows, crushed against walls... of toy poodles fragmented in the spin-dryer... 'The only thing for it,' he declared finally, 'is destruction.'

'I don't give one damn what you do with it,' said Teddy, 'as long as you get it outa here.'

'Well then, if you'd just lend me a hand to hump it down to the van...'

'Fuck you and it!'

The last he heard of Teddy was his mutton dummies on the stairs as he went to join the missus above.

Luckily all that chassying around had kept 'Dr. Who's' castors in good order and Jeffers managed to get it into the van without rupture. Elated, he headed for the Cut without bothering about the other call in Kilbraddock's. No need now; he doubted if Sanders would even enquire about anything else once he learnt about the captive rogue; triple-time was assured by the 1,000 word article that would blazen the name of Sanders across the middle fold of the trade magazine... The only reason Jeffers decided to do the remaining calls in the 'safe' part of Ballyturdeen was to put in time before returning to Belfast, where the daily bomb-scare traffic chaos would be at its worst.

As the Reservist had said, it was a private estate. Neat rows of semi-detached, chalet 'Dun Roamin's' with no sign of man, woman, child, dog or chimney smoke to denote human habitation.

At his first call the incontinent car in the driveway had a drip-pan underneath to save it soiling the virgin concrete. By a tiny artificial pool among the rose bushes a gnome (one of six) sat fishing, holding his rod, Jeffers noted with delight, at a most suggestive angle... It would be nice to think, he mused while awaiting an answer to his second thunderous knock, that whoever had purchased and placed that obscene dwarf had done so knowingly. But no, never, he decided, reading the varnished-crosscut-of-wood nameplate above the door...' Bali Hai.'

What first drew his gaze upward, Jeffers was to recall later, was the preliminary snick of the catch on the chalet bedroom window – like a cocked rifle-bolt in the stillness. Then the window wings flew outward, crashing against the brickwork on either side. The upper half of a woman fell out, waving its arms and making a noise like a small ship in a fog...

'Whoooooo... Whooooo...'

It had a ball-freezing effect on Jeffers similiar to that caused by the staircase scene in Hitchcock's 'Psycho.' He gasped up at the mad cuckoo in quilted pink and curlers, paralysed...

'Whoooooooo.. Whoooooooo.. Bomber...'

All around dogs began to bark, doors slammed, men's voices rumbled...' Whooooooo... bomber... Whoooooooooo...'

All around chalet windows opened and other female throats joined in...

'Whoooooooooo... bomber...'

But it was a man's voice, close at hand, that brought Jeffers out of his terrified trance. Whirling round he saw a big man in simmit and dangling braces running down the driveway of the house opposite. The big man shouted again – 'Git him, boys!' – and two dogs, one an Alsatian furred at the neck like a lion, the other a Dobermann pinscher, hurdled the hedge and came for Jeffers... Jeffers, his back to Bali Hai's front door, looked wildly round as other doors opened to disgorge other men in police tunics, khaki tunics, combat coats; one brandishing a shot-gun, another ramming a magazine in a Sterling...' Whoooooooooooooo...'

Jeffers ran. The dogs caught him half-way across the lawn, the Alsatian by the forearm, the Doberman by the ankle, spreadeagling him and beginning a grisly, snarling tug-o-war over his body. He heard himself screaming 'Spinduo! Spinduo!' over and over as the dogs wheeled him round and round on the close-shaven grass. And all around a blur of darkgreen legs, khaki legs, camouflaged legs as the men tried to get the dogs off him... Eventually they did – but only by dint of clubbing the Alsatian senseless with a pistol butt and rapping the pinscher on his fulsome testicles.

The men hauled Jeffers to his feet and held him propped between gun muzzles as he babbled 'Spinduo... Spinduo service...' The women and children had descended now and were crowding in all around, waving hammers, hatchets, kitchen cleavers (and one pair of nutcrackers, Jeffers was to recollect in tranquility), all howling, 'Bomber, bomber give him to us!... Killin's too good for him!' etc. But presently, the dog-owner, whom Jeffers recognised by his simmit and braces, spotted the firm's name on his overalls and shouted, 'Here, wait'll I have a dekko at that van...' And all the while Jeffers was being poked and pushed, one berserk lady managing to stretch over the phalanx of menfolk and grab a handful of his hair, tugging tenaciously...

The dog-owner swam back into vision, shouting and gesticulating – 'Lave him be, Cynthia. He's only a washing machine man.' – and the tension on Jeffers'scalp eased. The crush of bodies around him loosened and he sank down on the grass. The whooping faltered – but then... a lone, chilling soprano aria, 'He is, he is, he is...!' and, looking up, Jeffers saw Cynthia coming at him over the heads of the men, lips white with spittle, a brass toasting-fork in her fist... Just as the fork seemed inches from Jeffers' eyes the dogowner plucked Cynthia out of the air and subdued her with a neat right cross to the jaw. But the new screech rose in volume on all sides... 'He is, he is, he is!'

He came to briefly in a speeding, wailing ambulance and saw, in the stretcher opposite, a simmit and dangling braces...

During the following convalescent days the dog-owner (a police constable, from whose skull they were removing pieces of a Kenwood mixer) told Jeffers of the terrible scenes after he had passed out on the lawn. The men had formed square over his body and for half-an-hour had withstood a lynch-mob of their kith-and-kin. Visibly shaken by the memory, this veteran of Bogside battles described the fury with which ladies and offspring had flung themselves against the wall of breadwinners... He'd seen one man, a long service red-cap, being dragged out and garrotted while his 15 year old son had trampolined on his ulcerated gut; he was now in the intensive care unit. Another casualty had had his nose severed by a pair of hedge shears he himself had sharpened that morning... 'I'm tellin'ye,' said the dog-owner, 'if that patrol hadn't arrived with the C.S. we'd all have had it. That's one thing the bitches can't stand, the gas – it straightens their hair, y'see...'

Sanders came to visit with a bottle of Vichy Water and a copy of *'Fortnight.'*

'A monstrous fracas, Jeffers,' he said sternly. 'But I've managed to keep the company name out of the gutter press.'

'I thought maybe you'd bring me my pay,' complained Jeffers; 'they don't hand out fags on the National Health, y'know. I could do with some of that triple-time.'

'Triple-time!' Sanders laughed. 'For what, Jeffers? – provoking a riot? Oh, I'm not saying it was all your fault; but in cases like this there's always a contributing factor on both sides.'

'And what about the Dr. Who in the van? Eh? Isn't that –'

'– A Dr. Who! Come, come, Jeffers, your're not yourself yet. I collected the van from the police barracks this morning and l assure you that there was no Dr. Who or anything else in it. Pull yourself together, man.'

'Thievin,' fuckin' Peelers!' exclaimed Jeffers. 'I hope it ates them!'

JOHN MORROW

O'Fuzz

1976

'A TURRIBLE Booty is Born' I parodied to myself, after
O'Casey, surveying the splendour of it all: wall-to-wall vinyl
tiling; pneumatic armchairs with matching small table – for
coffee or feet – laden with confiscated stock, *Playboy*, *Knave*,
Armpit; discreet musak which at that moment was relaying,
appropriately, Eric Weissburg's banjo-picking from 'Bonny
and Clyde.' Approaching the enquiry aperture (really more a
proscenium arch, with subtle concealed lighting...and cameras?). I admired the open-plan, nothing-up-our-sleeves
design which allowed one, indeed pleaded with one, to view
the back wall of the building through a progression of glass
partitions. In the middle distance a face that could belong
only to a remanded mass-murderer pressed itself against the
glass, glowering – then turned away, swept a match on the
glass and began to light a pipe. It would demand all the
ingenuity of a dedicated sadist, I thought, to as much as
tramp on the toe of a suspect in this environment – forbye the
fact that one really heart-felt scream would mean everyone
up to his knees in shattered glass.

I pressed the enquiry button and was at once confronted
with as near Miss Ireland as I've seen in the flesh: auburn
curls, peaches and cream – with freckles – a starched blouse
bursting with goodies... 'Can I help you, Sir?' she asked,
genuinely concerned.

Anywhere else, even the Labour Exchange, I'd have told
her candidly just what help she could render me, always remembering the success story, occuring three thousand feet

above the Irish sea, of a friend and his unspoken reply to an ingenuous hostess's 'Can I lend a hand Sir?' But I knew that Policewoman R69 (as God's my judge!) would be just as likely to bound across the counter and try out on my soft parts all the nasty things she'd been taught at training depot, so I told her straight...

A small advert in the previous evening's paper had offered parts for a 1961 Morris van. The address given was a town-land in the Ards (the name escapes me now, but it was long and glottal, half-roads between a Gaelic battle-cry and a Planter's curse). In which direction did it lie? I wanted to know, it being in the area served by this station.

R69 rolled the strange name on her lovely tongue for a moment. 'No... I can't say I've ever heard... Wait, we'll try this...' She produced a book from under the counter and be-gan to run a rose-coloured fingertip through it. It was a postal codes directory, but suddenly the phrase 'Day Book' loomed in my mind and I remembered the last time I had cause to visit a police barracks – the day we lost Jimmy Gurney's corpse...

'No, I'm afraid it's not here,' sighed R69, pouting de-liciously. 'Well, look, it's O.K.' I said. 'I'll have a tootle around and ask –.' 'No, no,' she almost shrieked, brown eyes wide with pleading. 'That's what we're here for. These new code books can't be trusted, anyway; the post office seems to be making up their own names as they go along. So if you'll just take a seat for a minute I'll get on the R/T and ask some of the mobiles if they know... Please...'

It would have taken a heart of stone to refuse her. If I'd told her I had the Cockney burglar McStiofain dead and stuffed in the back of the van she couldn't have been more delighted. She scuttled into the room at the back of the counter and be-gan shouting things like 'Roger,' 'Charlie' and 'Bravo' into a radio hand-set.

I went over to the porn-laden coffee table and sat down.

There was a girl on the cover of *Armpit* who seemed about to do something quite extraordinary with a Kojak lollipop and I was reaching out for it, intending to see if the experiment was continued within, when I became conscious of the fact that I was being watched. Looking up, I met the unwavering stare of the pipe-smoking, remanded mass-murderer. He had moved much closer, only two partitions of glass now separating us. Armoured glass, I assured myself; but there was something in that censorious gaze that made a browse in *Armpit* unthinkable, so instead I thought of Jimmy Gurney's lost corpse while I waited...

One wet Tuesday in 1923 Jimmy had come in on a farm cart from Drumaness, bound for America. Late that same night, Mrs. Lizzie Tumath had found him sitting on her garden wall, drunk and drenched, all adventure spent. Lizzie, a war widow, had given him a bed, had gone with him the very next morning to sign him on the dole and, that same day, had guided his X on a proposal form for a shilling policy naming her as beneficiary (she was sure he'd never get over the drenching). Which was where I came in, forty years later, as an insurance agent collecting that weekly shilling.

Lizzie, on that second day when Jimmy was booting on death's door, had made the mistake of trying to grease the latch for him with a bumper of hot red biddy. One gulp kindled the coal in Jimmy, and there and then he decided to stay - though on a day to day basis, depending on the availability of the elixir.

When I first met him he was sixty-eight years of age, his face was Prussian blue and he smelt like the Out-patients in the Royal, inflation having long ago driven him to the Meths and worse. It was a bad tin of Kiwi dubbin, melted in hot water with sugar added, that finished him off in July, 1965.

I was on holiday when it happened, and I returned to find Lizzie Tumath camping on my doorstep with the shilling policy in her claw.

'Poor Jimmy's gone,' she keened, eyes streaming. 'Where?' I asked, knowing bloody well where. 'Back to Drumaness? They'll never have him after all this time.'

'Now none of yer smart Aleck stuff wi'me,' screeched Lizzie, suddenly businesslike. 'I've had dealings with youse graveyard bookies before. Yer not gonta flannel me outa my money this time.'

'Where's the death certificate?' 'I dunno. The Peelers came an' took him away an' that's the last I heard or seen of them or him... But he was as dead as mutton.'

Jimmy had been dead in his room for three days before Lizzie smelt him (when I queried this, wondering in what way the smell of death differed from Jimmy's normal odour, she said it had been like opening a cupboard full of old mouldy boots). And when Lizzie had gone screaming into the street in the traditional way a police patrol car had just happened to be passing. They had radioed for an ambulance, collected Jimmy's bits and pieces of personal things and that's the last Lizzie saw of them or Jimmy.

So it was up to me to find out what had happened to Jimmy's corpse and who had certified death. (If death, in fact, had occurred; the petro-chemical vintages have been known to cause a condition called 'Temporary Death,' a classic case being that of a Brasso victim in the Short Strand who sat bolt upright in his coffin and snatched a bottle of stout from the lips of a wakeing relative.) Having ascertained the barrack to which the police patrol belonged, I called in to enquire with some trepidation, knowing how they felt about intruders...

At that time the duty room in every urban police barracks had a billiard-hall atmosphere, consisting mainly of plug tobacco and male B.O. plus a nuance of Sloan's liniment; a place where heavyweight boxers, shot-putters and javelin hurlers put in time between training sessions. (Non-athletes were exiled to places like Fintona). There was always one man with his tunic on, the duty-man who dealt with the odd enquirer at the minute hatchway – though he, I suppose, could have been trouserless. The rest lounged about in various stages of undress, from shirt-sleeves through simmit and braces, to the occasional dressing-gown. They sprawled in armchairs, sat on tables or held up walls, all exuding an aura of dozy well-being. The general impression, I'd often thought, was that of a crew of shipwrecked stokers taking their ease in the fo'castle of the rescue vessel – except, that is, for the row of .45 elephant guns hanging by their trigger guards from a rack on the wall.

The duty man on that day was a fellow, not long out of the depot by the look of him; but he had learnt a trick or two already. For instance, when I rapped the hatch – causing a sudden silence within – and he stuck his head out, he didn't say 'Can I help you Sir?' or even 'Yes?' He said 'Well?' in a manner which left no doubt that the next, unspoken phrase was – 'What have you been up to?' The motley of athletes in the background glowered at me and flexed their biceps.

I explained my problem. His response was another question: 'What business is that of yours?' The biceps stirred approvingly. I told him, whereupon he grinned, glanced over his shoulder and said: 'Well, you'll hardly find your man here!' The biceps shuddered with mirth.

'Yes, I realise that,' I said evenly. 'But perhaps you could tell me to which hospital or morgue he was taken. Your men must have kept a record mustn't they?'

I could see that nobody liked my tone of voice. Obviously the depot had not prepared the lad for such repartee, for he flushed up, recoiled a step back from the hatch and then looked towards the biceps appealingly. From these there erupted a rumble of growls out of which I discerned the phrase 'Day Book.' The lad ducked down behind the hatch and came up with a grubby double-entry ledger which I could see was ruled five days to a page.

'When was it, you said?' he asked. 'Last Wednesday afternoon about three o'clock.'

It took three minutes of thumb licking and page turning to find last Wednesday. A triumphant cry issued from the lad as he stabbed a blank space with his forefinger... 'There y'are – nothing.'

'Nothing at all happened last Wednesday?' I asked incredulously.

'See for yourself,' he said contemptuously, swirling the book round. I saw that not only had nothing happened on Wednesday but also that Monday, Tuesday, Thursday and Friday had been equally unfull of events.

'Try back...' This, accompanied by a gust of Old Crowbar, made the both of us jump. Unnoticed by us a large grey man fully clothed in withered tweed had sidled up to the lad's elbow. His presence, I could see, unnerved the lad. 'Yes sir,' he said, and his hand trembled slightly as he began to leaf through the book. 'Sir' leant over his shoulder, now and then trapping a turning page with the stem of his pipe to read an entry. And each time, I noticed, a small puddle of brown spittle trickled from the mouthpiece onto the page. It was just as well there weren't very many entries in that book; one hour's good drying and it would have been as solid as a brick.

'Here!...' cried the lad suddenly, pointing. They both perused the entry. 'Sir's' pipe voided its most extensive deposit yet. Then the lad looked up and said to me: 'Here's two oul maids gassed themselves in Botanic Avenue, Wednesday, three weeks ago?'

That question mark is no slip of the pen. He was asking.

'Sir' straightened up, replaced his pipe between his teeth, and they both stared at me, awaiting my reply. I knew I had been checkmated. Certainly I could turn on my heel and walk away; but any reply I made now would trigger the inevitable denouement. Half in admiration of their cunning, I decided to go the whole hog.

'You mean,' I said quietly, 'that I can have the two old maids instead of Jimmy Gurney?'

You could see the tension go out of them. The lad gave something like a sigh and 'Sir' grunted contentedly, applying a match to his dead pipe. They looked at one another for a moment, and then 'Sir' nodded and turned away as if to say 'It's your case, son.'

The lad was on sure ground now. He closed the Day Book with a resounding splash; he reached up and took the edge of the hatchway shutter in both hands; he fixed me with an icy stare...'None of yer oul lip now,' he said in a voice loaded with practised menace and a good octave deeper than his normal key. He then banged the hatch closed...As I walked away, beaten, but with an odd feeling of satisfaction, I heard an outburst of applause from inside the duty room.

Eventually I found the still glowing remains of Jimmy Gurney in the City Hospital morgue and gave him such a slap-up funeral that there was very little of the claims money left over for Lizzie Tumath...

Meanwhile, back in the New Look '70's, the remanded mass-murderer had submerged behind the glazing again. I reached for *Armpit*...

'Hello... Sir... I say, Sir...'

It was R69 at the counter, beckoning. I rose and obeyed – at the same time, a completely unconscious action, folding and stuffing *Armpit* into my hip pocket.

'I'm sorry to keep you,' she said breathlessly; 'but I'm waiting for a reply to your query from one of our mobiles. He's asking someone down the peninsula' – '– It's not really worth the bother,' I protested.

A crackle of verbal static arose from the radio room... 'That'll be him now' cried R69, already in flight.

In her path between counter and radio room there was a door, a narrowish door leading onto a corridor, and once through it she had to negotiate a sharp left-hand turn. She was in process of doing this, at top speed in Charlie Chaplin fashion, with one foot in the air while performing a sort of hopping skid on the other, when something extraordinary occurred. From nowhere, out of the floor it seemed, a hand and arm appeared. It swept up and under R69's short skirt from behind, catching her at the very apex of her manoeuvre, causing her to shriek and topple away out of my view... But almost at once she was back framed in the doorway, little fists clenched on hips, stamping her foot, blushing madly and fairly spluttering with rage – all directed at some presence in the corridor hidden from me... 'Sergeant... you're... oh you're an awful...'

Then he was in the doorway, filling it, my remanded mass-murderer!... tired tweed with oxter bulge, brown boots, Old Crowbar... Oh God!

'Who's this?' he growled, meaning me, paying no heed at all to R69's anguished bleating. He lumbered over to the counter, looking as if poised to vault it if I broke and ran... I caught a whiff of that sweaty-sheep smell that arises only from long-johns at that stage of fission just before they have to be amputated. He took the pipe from his mouth and flicked it, projecting a jagged trail of spittle onto the dove-coloured floor.

'He's only looking for directions,' said R69 protectively, making a face behind his back. 'He wants to get to –,' she spoke the name of the townland.

'Is that all he wants! Sure that's easy,' said the sergeant. Then he addressed me: 'And who would you be wanting up that way, Billy?'

'My name isn't Billy,' I replied, moving my first pawn in a game, I knew, doomed to end the one way possible.

'Oh, isn't it... Well, anyway, I'll tell you the best way to get to that particular quarter. Just you drive about two miles out on the north road, stop at the first unmarked crossroads, get out of the car, shout 'up the Rebels!' and before you know it that place you're looking for will come looking for you.' He laughed and waves of Old Crowbar lopped over me. R69 smiled obsequiously. 'Eh...What d'you think of that for a joke, Paddy? I'm thinking of sending it to the papers.'

'My name isn't Paddy,' I stated recklessly.

'Ah sure we'll get to know your name soon enough; that's part of the joke, y'see,' he said jovially. 'Is that oul van outside yours? – the one with no tax disc, baldy tyres all round, one headlamp gone and the handbrake cable trailing on the road?'

I nodded philosophically.

'You'll be sorry to hear that it's been towed to the pound for further investigation. I wouldn't be surprised if they found bits of old people sticking in that front grill...' He turned to R69 and beamed. 'So there you are. Problem solved: he's not going anywhere so he doesn't need to know the direction of where he intended to go.'

R69 looked sheepish and avoided my eye. At that moment I had the chance to go, silently, and perhaps retain her sympathy. But, as before, I couldn't...

'Thank you, sergeant,' I said. 'I realize that it's all for my own good and that of the general public at large. And I know that you are only doing your duty in the finest tradition of the Irish Constabulary.'

He grinned and removed his pipe. Her eyes, suddenly wintry, met mine and they came in together on the cue like Jeanette McDonald and Nelson Eddy in 'Rose Marie'... 'None of yer oul lip now!'

Eoghan Ó Tuairisc was born 1919 in Ballinasloe, County Galway, Ireland. He has studied English, Irish, and the classics at University College, Dublin. After some years in the Irish Army and a long period teaching in Dublin, he retired to concentrate actively on creative writing in both languages. He has won many awards as a novelist, poet, dramatist, and short story writer, including the Irish-American Cultural Relations Prize (The Butler Award) for his novel of the 1916 Rising. He has developed the 'episodic novel,' close to the short story in technique, the first example of which is 'An Lomnachtan' (The Nude), published in 1977. (Mercier Press)

EOGHAN Ó TUAIRISC

The Blessed Wagtail

1976

IT WAS the Sunday of the closing of the Men's Mission. The Suck ran golden over the shallows, and lay like black glass clouded with midges in the deep hole near the Church. Old Tom's pace slackened. In his mind's eye that dark mirror of water seemed split by an upheaval, as the pike – the waterwolf – plunged mouth open for the bait. His forearm trembled, gripping an imaginary rod. In the left hand pocket of his jacket his dreaming fingers touched the hooks of his new bait. A wagtail. Two pieces of red rubber attached by snarewire to a brass swivel, and mounted with a pair of triple hooks. He had sat up late the night before, making it. He felt it would be a killer.

Dong! the bell boomed, recalling him to thoughts of the next world and the closing of the Men's Mission. He hurried on. When he had crossed the footbridge to the Market Square he met Eels Curley, his boat companion. Every Sunday, the pair of them set off after the pike, in the flatbottom boat which they kept moored in the reeds of the Convent Osiery; but only a pagan would go fishing on the Sunday of the closing of the Men's Mission. Dr. Mills, who was Church of Ireland, observed a gentlemen's agreement to regard that Sunday as an excluded day, and even Isaac Murphy the Pawnbroker forebore to cast a surreptitious bait upon the water.

'Well, Tom,' greeted Eels, 'did you make the wagtail?'

'No more o' that,' growled Tom. 'At a time like this a man should be thinking of his immortal soul.'

From all sides the men, in shining Sunday boots and stiff

collars, were pouring into the Square at the bottom of which the Church stood in a bend of the river Suck. Old Tom and Eels Curley joined the throng. At the standing before the Church gate they bought a blessed candle apiece. In addition, old Tom bought a rosary beads and Eels a medal showing the Miraculous Draught of Fishes. They elbowed their way into the crowded Church, and secured their favourite seat at the back of the side-aisle, where the bottom panel of a stained-glass window showed a miniature Jonah in the mouth of a magnificent whale.

'Fifty pounds if he's an ounce!' murmured Eels.

But Tom's bare bald head remained bent, pious, un-answering.

The Missioner, a bearded Franciscan, climbed into the pulpit, paused, then hurled his voice into the deathly stillness till each man felt under his ribs the reverberation of the last trumpet sounding his soul to eternity. An hour later, he ceased. In the unearthly silence they could hear the river harping on the shallows behind the Church. They sang a hymn, *O Lord, within thy nets are we*, Eels with his thin face puckered into a melodic agony, Old Tom in his cracked bass. They lit their candles, held them aloft, while the entire con-gregation in a moment of flaming enthusiasm renounced the Devil with all his works and pomps. Then the Missioner announced that he would bless their pious objects if they held them up.

Eels produced his medal. Old Tom fumbled for his rosary beads. His fingers met the barbed hooks of the wagtail. Temptation was swift, irresistible. He held the five-inch bait aloft by its swivel, shielding it with his big palm. Eels caught the glint of brass out of the corner of his eye, looked askance, saw a dangling triple hook. He blinked.

The Missioner raised his hand above them all, and in the immemorial Latin called down the blessing of the Omni-potent upon their statues, pictures, rosaries, images, medals, prayer-books, scapulars – and upon the five-inch wagtail which old Tom Harty in his cottage above the river had fashioned with painstaking fingers.

The nose of the flatbottom moved out on the river from its niche among the reeds. When it was in the clear, old Tom set the oars on the tholepins, while Eels on the fishing seat assembled the gear. It was the Sunday after the closing of the Men's Mission, a morning early in October, and the Suck was veiled in a shallow mist out of which the upper parts of the reeds and alders emerged into the pale sunshine.

Ideal for the pike.

Tom turned the nose with a sweep of the offside oar, and headed upstream. Eels mounted the wagtail on a short steel trace, drew off thirty feet of line from the wheel, and cast over the stern. Hardly had the bait nicked the surface of the water when there came a savage plunge, and the jaws of the water-wolf snapped shut with a clash of teeth that rang like a pistol shot in the windless air. Eels struck with such force that the greenheart rod bent double in his grasp. Sharp and fierce the fight raged, from side to side of the river. But with Tom skillfully handling the oars, and Eels skillfully handling his wooden wheel, the pike was at length fought to a finish. Eels drew alongside, old Tom reached for the gaff, and with a swift thrust had the waterwolf on board.

'Nine pounds if he's an ounce,' declared Eels, measuring the fish with an expert eye. 'Be the powers, Tom, that blessed wagtail is a killer!'

That was the beginning of a memorable day. Going under the Red Bridge they collected half a dozen small jack in Jones's Cut, and made a massacre among the pike that infested Heartbreak Hill. And by the time they went ashore at Ballygill Bridge to drum-up, they had seventeen fish on the bottom of the boat.

They lit a fire of hazel branches, boiled the kettle, made tea,

ate their meal of bread and roasted onions, then sat awhile
smoking placid pipes by the river's brink in the mild autumn
sunshine, thinking deep thoughts as they gazed on the deep
water.

'Latin is a strange language, Tom.'

'It's not altogether the language that does it. It's some
power given to the monks when they're made missioners.
Sort of, – Go ye therefore...'

Their journey home through the gathering dusk was even
more remarkable. Eels had the oars now, and old Tom with
trembling incredulous hands manoeuvred the rod and line.
He fought a monster pike for twenty minutes in the
Derrymullen Perch-hole, and collected a sizeable jack at the
Cursed Corner where no one had ever caught a fish within the
memory of man. And as he cast the bait again into the
mingled mist and dusk of the evening, he knew that this was
no ordinary wagtail, but a wagtail that had some strange
virtue in it which no pike in the river could resist.

Dark was already fallen on the air by the time they returned
to their moorings in the niche among the reeds. They had
forty-odd fish in the boat, so that she was down to her
gunnels in the water, The biggest was over seventeen pounds,
the smallest was no bigger than a pencil-case.

Eels hurried home for his handcart. The word spread far
and wide about the town of Lisanackedy, and a crowd collected to see the miraculous draught. They formed a procession behind the handcart as Eels pushed it to the Market
Square, to the strains of a melodeon and by the light of
blazing sods of turf carried aloft on pitchforks. It was a night
of nights, the greatest single haul of pike that had ever been
known in the memory of man. They proceeded to the Market
Bar. Drinks all round. Dr. Mills from the Lunatic Asylum and
Barkley the Bankmanager weighed each fish with a spring
balance, and wrote an account of the event and the date, and

signed their names, that it might be recorded forever in the annals of our Town. And Isaac Murphy bought the bulk of the catch at fourpence a pound.

In the few years of life that were left him, old Tom Harty took extraordinary care of his blessed wagtail. He chose a special tobacco-tin for it – *Mick McQuaid Cut Plug*; and he kept the box wrapped in oiled silk in his fishingbag. He never fished it except as a last resort. On one of those dull and dreary days, when the alderleaves hang limp above the sullen water, and even the dabchicks doze like feathery little balls of soot among the rushes, when some wicked spell lies like a faint scum on the river and everything fails to attract the waterwolf, then, on such a day, old Tom would unwrap the silk and open the precious box and mount the wagtail. Never once was it know to fail. The bait would snick the water, the plunge would come, the spell of the Suck would be broken.

As for the wagtail, it suffered a good deal of wear and tear in the jaws of innumerable pike; but when he thought to repair it, adding fresh wire and new hooks, he found that it lost all its virtue. He restored it, therefore, to the original state in which it had been blessed by the Missioner: the virtue returned, and so it continued till the day he died.

On his deathbed, the Canon found him resigned. He had had a long life, his share of hard work, and more than his share of the Sunday fishing. 'And Canon,' he murmured with his last breath, 'maybe I'll see Saint Peter, another oul fisherman. Maybe when it comes to the pinch in the place beyond, he won't see a riverman stuck.'

He had left clear instructions with Eels that the wagtail in its box was to be buried with him. And when they carried his coffin through the graveyard gates, within sight of our greyeyed well-beloved Suck, Eels Curley and Isaac Murphy and Dr. Mills and Barkley the Bankmanager – fishermen all – they had a sad thought for old Tom Harty, and a sad thought

for the blessed little wagtail that was going down forever into
the obscure grave.

It was Eels told me the story. One afternoon on the river. I
was home in Lisanackedy for the holidays and he was rowing me in the old flatbottom along the pike-reaches of the
Upper Suck. One of those dreary days. Thunder in the air.
The water was the colour of wet lead, and we had travelled all
the way up to Croffy's Island without the smell of a fish. We
drummed up on the Island, boiled the ancient black kettle on
the ritual fire of hazelwood, had our meal of tea and roasted
onions. It had to be onions: I had learned by then that it was a
kind of sacrilege to bring anything else when pikefishing on
the Suck. And while we sat and smoked among the crumbling
stones and thyme by the river's brink, Eel told me stories of
the days gone by.

We slipped downstream in the still evening. The old boat
rode the current like a bird. Beyond the reddening boglands,
the spire of Lisanackedy church lay pencilled on the skyline.
Six o'clock. But at this distance the evening bell was no more
than a memory. I had lost all interest in the silver spoon I
trolled behind the boat, my mind drifted off, pondering the
complexities of the human spirit, and all the rivermen that
had rowed down this reach in the drift of the everliving,
irrecoverable years.

We were abreast of the Derrymullen Perch-hole. Eels
shifted on his haunches, muttered to himself:

'Desprit diseases needs desprit remedies.'

Letting the oars hang from his armpits, he fumbled in his
bag, drew out an old tin box. He prized it open.

'Here, young fella me lad. Try this for a change.'

I took the bait. A brass swivel rusted green with age, two
shreds of rubber, a pair of halfeaten triple hooks hanging by
the merest threads of wire.

'Looks as if it might have been a wagtail once,' I said, dubi-

'Young fella...that's the girleen herself.'

In silence the boat glided through the hazel fuzz, entering the Perch-hole; the oarblades hung like wings suspended.

'But Eels...look, I thought you said you buried it in his coffin?'

'Well?' Eyes in a thin, puckered face looked mournfully out at me. 'The divil tempted me, young fella. I couldn't find it in me heart to let that blessed thing go down into an earthly grave. The night of oul Tom's wake I abstracted it from his box, and put a common wagtail o' me own in its place. Aye. But when the trumpet sounds on the last day out, oul Tom will wake and look for his Wagtail, and then the fat 'll be in the flamin' fire. However, that might be a long time off yeat. Try out that bait now, avic, and may the Man Above be good to us all!'

I mounted the thing to humour him, fastened the swivel to the split ring of my trace. It was a sorry object, time-broken as the hands which had fashioned it, and which now in the earth were no more than nerveless claws of inarticulate bone. I released the catch of my latterday spinning wheel, and cast the poor relic in under the grass-weed at the edge of the pool. There was an unmerciful snap. All hell at once broke loose. It took all my strength to hold the rod, and Eels was hard put to it to hold the boat against the plunge and drive of the mighty fish. Half an hour of time and half a mile of water the fight lasted. Every reedclump in sight was set in motion, the floating leaves of waterlilies were tossed and tangled as if in the wake of a passing barge. Eels cursed and prayed under his breath, the wheel's ratchet whined and sang, my heart thumped, the veins were swollen on my aching wrists; but the line held, the ancient wire of the Wagtail, as if by miracle, defeated the berserk fury of the waterwolf. At last, double-hauling on the rod, I brought him alongside. His back stayed upright to the very end. Eels, the perspiration dripping from under the peak of his cap, got the gaff in his gills, and it took the two of us all our time to haul him aboard.

There he lay, the grim jaws of him, the streamlined body patterned of silver and black and green, the lovely fantail twitching, the protruberant eyes.

'Twenty pounds if he's an ounce,' muttered Eels, taking an iron bar to brain the monster. 'Praise be to the Man Above, young fella, but one day the two of us will roast alive in hell for this.'

EOGHAN Ó TUAIRISC

Per Ominy Ah

1975

—LOOKAT THAT fella, said Rosaline, floating along on his altarshoes like holy God. —He's nice, Myra said, her look lingered on the fair head passing below, so neat and innocent, made her feel what they doing was lowclass, but it wasn't a Sin.

—Nice me ah, said Rosaline. She took a couple of green alderberries in her mouth, put the shank of hemlock to her lips, shot. Myra saw the boy wincing, it must have stung him on the ear, he stood looking up and about in the dazzle of evening sunlight under the Earl's trees. Their two heads ducked down, they giggled, ducked quickly up again to peep.

—He's gone on. Wouldn't you just love to take that sur-plice and soutane from under his oxter and do a bellywobble dance in it? —It's lovely on him on the altar, but. All starch and ironed and the lace dripping six inches from the sleeves and skirt. —Love to muck it up, said Rosaline. She shot aim-lessly at a couple of people going down the long street that is all to one side to Evening Benediction.

The last of the footsteps had ceased on the path, they were alone in the attic above the emptiness of the street. Myra lay on the bed, floating, the danger was like an itch under her girdle. Had never done this before. Knew Rosaline some-times mitched from Sunday Benediction. Always gone her-self, with the girls from her end of the Town, liked it, the incense, white surplices on the shoals of altarboys, the Latin hymns. —What'll we do now, Rose?

—Scratch everything. She began walking and speeching, her trick since she had been in the Play, about here they were, another summer evening melting away in the attic with the dolls, the picturebooks, the sunbeam patterns through the lace curtains of her childhood, scratch it all she wasn't a child, fifteen, thin as one of those bloody peashooters, she flung it out the window. Myra might guess what was eating her, those glasses, the boys called her Foureyes, ruined from reading, the best in the class at everything, but not Music, nearly all those books were prizes, her people couldn't buy them, a shovel-man on the Railway and a bit lowclass too her Mum always said, living on the Hill where there was Morcheen Dead the lavatory cleaner, and gillygollies, don't let me catch you going up there, Myra—

—Them fellas have all the fun, dressing up like dotes in lacy skirts and swinging the incense thing. And let go right up on the altar. —But the Nuns can go right up— —Scratch the Nuns, it's a bit of religion I want, not Nuns. —But I thought you didn't— —Fat lot you thought. Scratch it all, life is more than lollies and Nuns' prayers and practice-hops with those numbskull know-alls scratching your backside at the Parochial. Myra laughed, but she knew it was something that shouldn't be talked about, not ladylike to let on you noticed even though it was nice, and you didn't have to tell it in Confession because Sister Alacoque didn't put it on the list.

—I want to do something, sacrifice something, sort of.

—Such as what?

—Don't know. She was standing by the shelf where her dolls were arranged, most attractive in the attic, blondes and brunettes with shining faces, long eyelashes, they were dressed in satin, watered silk, lace over brocade, it was Rosaline's passion to make them, old wrecks of dolls she got anywhere, she painted their lips and cheeks. She took one of them by the hair of the head and dashed it against the wall.

—I want to do something really firstclass wrong. Myra

watched the green eyes uneasily, Rose was working up, she was afraid she might want them to undress and go to bed, what the Boarders had been expelled for, Seniors, everyone knew, though it was put out it was for ducking the Night Prayers.

—I want to do something real, something primitive. She was dangling another doll by the leg like as if she meant to send it sailing out the window. —Rose dear, said Myra, she felt her voice thicken in her throat, —would you like for us to go to bed? —Kidstuff. All right for Mammy's big little pets afraid to grow up. No, I'll tell you what we'll do—

Appeared there was a fierce life of their own in the long fingers, they snatched the case off a pillow, rammed the doll into it, then doll after doll was grabbed from the shelf, black African dolls, Red Indian dolls, Spanishees, bridal, strip-tease, sailor dolls, one after another they were packed into the pillowcase. Myra grew afraid of her, she looked queer, re-mote was the only word for it, maybe she was bewitched for ducking the Benediction.

—Move yourself, kitten. Pack that other pillowcase. And we'll pile in a load of those silly books, God, sight of them makes me sick. Reluctantly Myra got off the bed and began to take down books—*Tanglewood Tales, Freda in the Fourth, St. Brigid of Ireland.* 'Presented to Rosaline McAnally...' She was in School out of charity, they called it a scholarship, but the charity didn't cover hockey skirts or Music, Sister Alacoque had it in for her since the day she put the Hallowe'en mask on the statue, sacrilege, slapped before the whole School, but really it was very impressive, the horrible face, she should have been expelled, would too only they wanted her to get good marks for the School in the Examination. Lord, she was tearing down the half of the lace curtain. —Golly, your Mum won't half be laxative when she comes back from the Chapel. Why tear the curtain? At full stretch reaching up she tore down the second one. —There has to be lace in this kind of thing.

Next thing they were downstairs with the loaded pillow-slips crossing the empty kitchen to the backdoor. Rosaline said, —Wait. She filled a saucer of milk, set it on the floor, hunted in the stairhole till she found a sack, opened the door a slit and began, —Pishwishwish. Here Tom-ee! The ginger cat, it was the poor Collins' from next door, da on the dole, padded in, flicked his tongue into the milk. Next was nightmare. A flurry of ginger fur, spitting and clawing, Rosaline's long fingers had him gripped by the scrag of the neck. —Hold the sack, eejit! Myra was paralysed, she saw the curved nails, naked, flash bright and quick, blood welled from Rosaline's sliced wrist, all by herself she held the sack open with the bleeding hand, slammed the snarling ginger into it with the other. —Quick, tie it— no, not me hand, eejit, the sack. With fumbling fingers Myra tied some sort of a knot, she was faint at the sight of blood dripping on the lino. Whitefaced, Rosaline sucked the wound, like a boy, spat into the slop-bucket, ransacked the hot-press for a bit of cloth to tie it up, at high speed, Myra had only half an eye for her, her whole attention was on the sack on the floor jerking of its own accord, daft, she was half deciding to run out the front door and never stop till she was safe inside the Chapel, hat or no hat. In a daze she found herself following Rosaline out.

Out into absolute quiet. Backyard in shadow, not a dog barked, in the whole long street of houses smoking up the length of the Hill no one was alive except the very old people and babies, all were gone to Benediction, not of course Morcheen Dead who never darkened a Chapel door, and there were a few Protestants. There was gold in the glitter of rainwater drops on the cabbages, they went down the garden path crouched close to the hedge shouldering the pillowcases packed, in her other hand Rosaline dangled the sack at arm's length, but it was quiet. Myra walked tense, excited too, it was like walking out of the real world, just like Rosaline, an odd kind of wickedness nobody else would think–they would now be putting the sweet grains in the incense thing, thurible, Hughdy swinging it on long silver chains, everybody singing 'Jenny Tory, Jenny Toe-o-kway,' she could hear them, nearly, but the spire of the Chapel was out of sight behind the Monniment, trees, good thing too. What now? She followed Rosaline over the rusty tangle of wire and weeds at the bottom of the garden out into the boreen. Filthy, no one ever went there, just a dump for the Hill houses, slops, ashes, tin cans, unspeakabilities, she picked her steps, her white ankle-socks were ruined, Rosaline had black wool socks to the knee, through a tangle of buttercups grown fat on the rot, hemlocks head-high, ranks of nettles that would give you gooseflesh the very look of them, and the old greynettle breath, feel like you had lice in your hair, till Rosaline stopped at a wall. She flung the sack up and the pillowcase and began climbing.

—Oh Rose, not there. It's the Monniment.

—Of course it's the Monniment. That's why. Throw me up your bundle.

Legs trembling she climbed up into the forbidden place. A slope of grass between darkish trees, the poisonberry trees, air stink with them. And there it was, the Thing, the stonework was all spattered with white scum, there were these pillars tall and thin with a stone coffin thing between them, a tree sprouted from the roof, dome, it was the shape of a Pagan temple some people said, built for a dead Earl, haunted — but it wasn't the Thing was the real itch in the air, it was the long silky grass all beaten down, rolled, here couples came, Lord, it crossed her mind, m'Mum'd have the britches offa m' bottom if she thought—

—Don't stand there gawking. Get sticks.

She went fumbling into the sharp tang of the trees, tried to keep her thought off it, grown-up couples are a sickening thing, all that grass rolled, she tried to say a prayer, Sister Mary Alacoque, for holy purity, but her mind was dazed, all she could think of was,— There are four corners on this bed.

There are four angels overhead—

She woke from this kind of a blank to find herself on her hunkers tearing pages from a picturebook and piling them on a fire, it was lit by the stonework at the butt of the Thing. Rosaline was taking books asunder, breaking their spines and clawing bunches of pages out of their bindings, and showering them pellmell on to the lick of the flames, they flared up over head-high and lit the little glade making a cosy corner in the dusk of the trees. Inside of the shadow everything was alive and lit with meaning. They had the lace curtains on, holes torn in them for the head so they draped down back and front like vestments, and they had sprays of leaves with the red berries in their hair. Rosaline said they were yew.

She took a doll near as big as a child in her arms, a red-cheeked beauty in winedark velveteen, her blue eyes could move. She dangled it over the flames and said like chanting,— Unto Thee do we hereby give thine servant Esmeralda. Per Ominy Ah sickala sickalorum. Now you say Amen. Myra murmured it. —No, you must sing it, like this,— Ah-meh-ehn. The doll dropped, the dimpling face melted immediately, you could feel for it, the fire singeing the hair and the dinky underclothes. Doll after doll went on the burning pile, each with a chant and a special prayer. The fire thickened, a mass of flames and yellow smoke, it clung to the stonework curling up, until the last doll, it was a little naked thing, a black baby, was kissed and given to Per Ominy Ah.

Trees, Town and all else were far on the mind's edge in the firelit circle. Myra, with Rosaline there, lived in a rich sense of herself, masked in the red light, the lipred berries and the lace. Palm to palm they danced, waltzed, did the foxtrot on the dry and slidy grass, sang,— Along the shores of Minnatonka where I left my love, Ah, Ho!— she floated in the banjo harmony of it, till Rosaline suddenly began to jerk and stamp in polka-time, took her by the waist, swung her with flaring heart over the edge of the fire. She screamed in delight. Wilder and bolder they grew in the dance with airborne lace and floating skirts and toes highkicking, now the one, now the other, screaming and spread-leg over the waft of the heat.

They sat on the grass out of breath, knees touching, not talking, staring into the heap of ash and embers, poking it with sticks to let the night-wind at it, making it glow. Black pages, curled and brittle, there were scraps of letters still to be seen on them in a ghostly grey trying to say words, they broke them to bits, and fragments of faces, charred limbs, tufts of halfburnt hair, and pairs of eyeballs hung on the wires that had worked them still bright and hard in the hot dust. Per Ominy Ah. Myra was half-asleep, her eyes glazed in the warm dream of it, when she heard Rosaline's voice say,— Time now for the Jenny Tory. She shivered. Rosaline daubed yewberries on their cheeks, blacked their eyebrows with paper-ash, then went from the red dusk into the dark. Myra wanted to say,— No! but couldn't. She came back, the sack dangled dead-weight from her hand held out, she walked with long strides that sent the lace floating back from her shoulders, her painted face was like a mask in the murk. She kicked the fire to flaming,— Sing! she hissed. She swung the sack to and fro over the fire in time to the drone of the hymn,— 'Jenny Tory, Jenny Toe-o-kway...' Myra felt a croak in her voice, flopped on her knees she was, couldn't stand, this was just that bit too insane. She tried to forget, but there it was, the sack coming alive as the heat licked it, it began to squirm and jerk, every snarl it gave sent a spasm of fright to the pit of her stomach, Stop! Stop! Oh Jesus me heart— She began to giggle, saw the bottom of the sack char, grow red, glow, split, the living tangle of claws and fur fell into the fire, sent a cloud of flame, sparks and hot dust in the air. Burning fur, the stink of it near blacked her senses out, a shape shot living from the lot, claws scrabbled on stonework, it streaked up the length of the Thing into the dark.

Rosaline lay on the ground in kinks. It was a while before it dawned on Myra that she might be weeping. She darted over and knelt beside her, put an arm round her. —There now, darling. The thin bony shoulders shook in her arm with every silent sob, the teeth were clenched, the raddled cheeks were a mess of ash and tears. Myra held her a long time while the dew fell cold about them and the fire died.

Photo by Colman Doyle

Lucile Redmond was born in 1949. She was brought up between Dublin, the Aran Islands, and California. She lived for a while in various communes, then returned to writing and won a Hennessy Literary Award with her first short story, 'The Shaking Trees,' in 1975. She has worked at a variety of jobs: playground supervision, gardening, teaching, research, printing, and journalism. Her grandfather, Thomas Mac Donagh, was a signatory of the Irish Declaration of Independence. In her distant literary background is her great-great-great-great-great uncle, Sir Richard Burton ('Arabian Nights' and the first English translator of the Kama Sutra).

LUCILE REDMOND

The Shaking Trees

Hennessy Literary Award, 1975

IT WAS a year for death, and the card of rebirth showed often in her Tarot. The old man on the corner said, shifting on his crutches, that 'happiness comes early or never,' but the swan who had her nest at the bend of the river would say 'he who implores the butterfly to rest lightly on him has had commerce only with falcons.'

She walked by the river every day, by the pine groves and down to where the tannery effluent poured its heavy mass into the glittering water. She avoided her own kind and they avoided her. Since Jimmy's death they seemed masks of skin on bone, and the time she spent talking to them was filled with silences. On a Thursday when the moon was rising she performed the conjuration of Vassago, but the images were unclear and the information phrased in symbols whose forms were distasteful to her. His deadness was unreal, and she was always surprised not to find him in the places where they had met. She had taken from his room some of his talismans; two car keys and an Ace of Spades, and occasionally she would take them out and look at them to see if they had changed, or perhaps if he had.

One day, as she sat by the swans' nest, reading the Book of the Dead to the cygnets, a boat came by. The man in the boat had features rounded into hardness.

—How deep is the water here? he asked.

It took a while for the question to reach her, and then some time while it bounced around the levels of her mind and came to rest as a thing of meaning. She considered it for some time, and then realised that it or its source required an answer.

—Shallow.

—You see I want to kill myself, the young man said with some satisfaction, but I can't find it deep enough.

The swan had returned with some reeds in her beak to patch the side of the nest, which had almost been swept away by the current, and she said indistinctly through them, When it is time to go, the path will show itself without questioning. The man in the boat paid no attention.

—The water by the tannery is deep and foul, whispered a rowan tree.

She pointed downstream, as the man loosed the branch he had been holding. The boat floated off with the current. She watched it go and returned to her reading.

It was soon after this, or perhaps it was not, but to her it seemed quite soon, that they cut down the pine forest. As she came near the river she could hear the sharp, dark buzzing of the saws, and as she came closer she heard the trees screaming. She walked through the cloud of sap and sawdust and on down to the town where the high walls of the slaughter house reeked with fear. In the clear water of the river the reds and browns and greens made steamy patterns. There were some boats with men dragging the bottom.

A week later the forest was gone and the hill was bleak with bleeding stumps. The cygnets were swimming now, and the cob had returned. She took out the talismans and found that a key was gone.

She had not eaten since the day Jimmy died, but at first drank sips of water whenever she began to tremble. Now she trembled all the time. The old man spoke of circles and haloes and she listened with the outside of her mind, not from politeness, but because he spoke in patterns. When she walked she performed as necessary the rituals of three and the laying of the patterns on the path, and spoke courteously to the older trees, because this was the custom. She began to feel cold even when the fish were basking at the surface of the water, and the small birds would perch near her to sing. Her skin felt transparent and fragile and she walked slowly, with care.

An aunt of Jimmy's came by one day and screamed at her.

—You killed him. You and these filthy things. She flung a handful of multicoloured tablets to the floor. The colours mingled and fused, flowing through each other, moving and changing. The woman was shaking her, and the sounds of her screams of rage and pain mixed and swirled like the colours on the floor. After a while she left, the tablets remaining as an offering.

She stooped and played with them, rolling them at each other like little skulls, running them through her fingers like pieces of eight, then she put them in her pocket with the remaining car key and the Ace of Spades and walked slowly down to the river. It was later than she usually came and there were men fishing. The swans hissed in a mannerly way as she sat in the hollow beside their nest, and a man turned, warning, and shouted at her. He lives on death and must die to live, the pen remarked sadly. The line of the fisherman's rod sprang taut and he began to fight, drawing in the line and loosing it with harsh grinding sounds, letting the fish run and drawing it back until he dragged it in and netted it. It whipped and writhed in agony while he watched it, smiling, then he grabbed its body and smashed the head against a rock, and tossed it into a pile of corpses on the grass. She watched for an hour as the silver of its scales dulled, then as the reflections of sunset filled the air with a red mist, she walked to the tannery, pausing often to breathe.

She discovered the aspens because she needed trees. She sat and trembled in the middle of the grove and did not feel she had to talk or listen. It was the first time in a long while that she had relaxed. Once in a while one of the trees would make a remark, and some time later one of the others might answer, or merely sigh.

The swans were cool when she next came by their nest.

—All is one in nothing, but everything has its right place, said the cob, looking closely at her. She was startled into answering, 'why?' and at the strange sound of her voice rose to run, but at the sudden movement merged into nothingness. When she woke she found the pen looking at her with a strange expression, mixing awe, sorrow, disgust, other emotions she could no longer name. The cygnets were milling curiously around, but the pen held her body between them and her. She stretched her arm into the water and felt its goodness flow through her. The Ace of Spades which she had been holding fluttered off down the surface of the stream.

The old man on the corner would not speak to her any more, and clumped into a doorway, humping along hastily on his crutches when she passed. He crossed himself, too, and called on images whose meanings were clouded, and almost transparent in her mind.

But the aspens were always there, and now the wind ruffled her as it did them. She liked to kneel on the scanty grass between them and hear the draughts humming quietly among them. Alone, she felt a longing for their company, and with them she was nourished and befriended.

When she went to the swans' nest only the cob was there, the pen and cygnets always seeming to be up the river or over the falls. He stretched his neck and tweaked gingerly at the tender green hairs that had begun to sprout on her arms.

She found that houses did not seem to like her, and would drop stones near when she walked, or change their shape so that she became lost and confused easily. She walked so slowly now that the dimensions of places seemed completely changed. She did not like to lose contact with the growing earth. After staying out all through one starry night she found it impossible to enter a house again and took to sleeping in the aspen grove or down by the river, or just lying and watching the moon glide through the clouds, the edge of the sky.

She learned the phases and humours of the moon and understood slowly how they affected the moods of the different trees.

That month she noticed that her blood had lost its colour and was a faint, opaque green. She had come to spend a lot of her time kneeling on the bare earth with her fingers threaded through the flesh of the clay.

The earth swirled slowly about her hands and the wind danced in her unfurling hair. The aspens laughed easily as the wind swayed their trembling bodies.

The swans' nest was empty. The season had changed. She did not know whether swans change their homes with the seasons. She asked the rowan tree, but it only whispered— below the falls the stream is fouled.

Walking by the wooden bridge she thought something, and stopped to consider what it was somewhere she knew. But she could only find after long searching, that something had happened, or used to happen by this place, but whether to her or to somebody or something she knew, she had no idea.

She was reluctant now to leave the green light of the grove. She knelt, her long fingers reaching down to the hidden streams, learning, always now talking sweetly with the stones and other sleeping things that lived below the grass roots. The moon played with her hair and it came to crinkle and stretch when it felt the first rays. She felt the subtle currents of warmth and moisture in the passing air, and she breathed her nourishment out for the animals that came to graze or nest among the still and trembling trees.

The season grew colder and the trees talked less often. Gradually a yawning silence spread through the grove. Sometimes small animals scuttled through the trees with amazing rapidness. Then it came that they moved so fast that they were like irritating buzzing. She wondered vaguely whether this was a seasonal change. She was too sleepy to bother reasoning it out. Her leaves began to itch at about the same time as the wind became gusty and blew them off in moulting tufts. She cradled the nests in her branchforks and hunched against the cutting gale. The snow blew to bank around her shivering trunk. She became warm and dozy. The aspens slept for the winter.

LUCILE REDMOND

Transients

1976

THAT SUMMER he seemed to drift through the city, fading from street to street, his pale fox's eyes always surprised at a meeting. He was to be seen sitting quietly by the canal, watching the swans, a hand held out across the water, and later in a bookshop his bony face would appear around a corner, pamphlets of poetry dropping from his limp hands. He had come from Chartres or Arles, one of the mystical cities, and in Dublin he was a ghost in Grafton Street.

It was a summer of processions and military parades, of humans losing humanity in mutuality, in symbiosis. The streets were forever thronged with rhythm, an eternal Mardi Gras haunted by the hollowed hands of Dublin's begging idiots. Brassy music floated from somewhere always, as if an army had been struck by plague and the death-carts were proceeding from house to house on their round to the graveyard, followed by a full dress military funeral. Seagulls voraciously circled the greyed skies. The rivers moved uneasily. Everywhere were roads dug up and deserted, workmen crouched around braziers, hands around enamel mugs, faces silently following the passers. Behind every hungry eye was a blacklist. A feeling of death brushed the city.

As he seeped around a corner the street before him cleared a way; he was thin, ragged, but with a bourgeois capability which edged on the nerves of people waiting for hunger. Each was isolated in a continuum of fear. These fading afternoons were remembrances of days in the cafés of youth, when there was hope.

They walked alone, stunned by the terrible loss of living; blocked from rightful joy by chosen pleasure. Children walked, eyes in poorly faces, incongruous in brightly coloured coats and anoraks. Poverty spread on the streets like a sickness.

The comfortable women of the moderately rich, their faces made up to conceal calculation, fled from interior to interior in shoes impractical as the bound feet of the ladies twittering in a Manchu court. They spoke correctly, according to formula. Nothing was new.

Everywhere one went he was, that summer, appearing around corners, sitting in parks reading. The graffiti on the walls that year spoke of anarchy and princes; *Hitler Kills King. Revolution is the Opium of the Proles. Women in Labour Keep Capitalism in Power.* Curly-headed boys and girls, factory-made in denims, lined the roads to the country, thumbs held out like the open beaks of nestling birds.

He used to eddy through the streets, watching smokily; one day he was in the red and black hell of a city hamburger joint, ravenously eating a bleeding hamburger and bronzed delicious chips. With him was a pale girl with hair as white and wild around her face as bog cotton. She had a shattered beauty. She watched the street below intensely, as if to catch it out in unreality, but turned back to him with a doubtful, trusting smile. He moved, disturbed under her wide gaze.

The streets cowered under a grinding of traffic. The city was like a woman eroded by the coldness of her man, yellow bulldozers everywhere coveting the black soil the skin of pavements kept concealed. Outside the Kildare Street Club the smell of bad and wholesome cooking and Irish prosperity spread on the air and bands of businessmen burst gaily from the doors and swung down the streets chatting in the warmth of full bellies, keeping up a noise to cover uneasy lines drooping on their faces.

He walked down Duke Street on a Friday afternoon with a

distempered pup in his arms, then stopped and pressed it on a person coming out of the Bailey, who brought it away in a car, while he went down the street alone again.

On a bright night he was in a late-night café, silent as usual and drinking tea. The girl with the white-flossed hair had taken to wearing black.

It was a time for propaganda, from the street singers and the television. A way of dressing or speaking became a flag.

A moustache made its appearance and he was dapper for a while. His face would appear for a moment in a crowd, distinguished by knowledge of him, and meld again into the broad mass of the lumpenproletariat.

It was a quarter to twelve—there was a man in a suit checking his watch—when he arrived, peering around the glass-and-wood tables at matrons discussing their hopes in their children. He sat and read a book in French, tattered almost to bits.

A weariness dulled the colours of the wallpaper, dragons imported from communist China tarnishing under the weight of hopes. A young man appeared and sat with him — the source of the moustache. They spoke, both intensely, yet not appearing to have full attention on the outside, seeming to drag a knowledge from manners or necessity.

The trees were green between blossom and fruit, the grass weary. Buses screeched and sighed. Couples came together and parted and came again together as if there was no other solution.

Summer dissolved slowly into autumn. Some of the old who wandered the streets disappeared. Young girls trod softly through the streets. A ship docked. Town was full of sailors in blue, eyes moving restless in stretched faces, hips tiny in wide blue trousers, arm around a willing waist, eyes that clinked and eyes that clung. Their accents were as strange as parrots. A word or two remained in the slang of the city.

The cafés were full of those men with eyes so much sadder

than those of the down-and-outs; dressed in jerseys under sports jackets, the collars of shirts pointing over their folded crewnecks, tweed sagging sorrowfully, they sat stirring sugar slowly into their coffees and looking out of their faces as if there was an answer. Down in the streets shuffled the no-hopers, coats tied with rope, exuberant day by day. It was still warm in the season of apples and they munched through the streets, eyes narrowing for the main chance. The clouds lowered.

The autumnal invasion of the headband hippies disturbed the streets in a swirl of Moroccan cloaks and lost ideals. The addicts stood deadeyed on the corners watching the students explore, waiting for their turn to come. The students walked as if the pavements were indeed solid.

His eyes clouded, he whirled through the city consulting maps of Europe. He sat with a group the first day cold enough for chocolate mary cakes.

'The mary cakes have returned!' He spoke, orgiastically. A map of Northern Spain was spread out on the table in front of him, his goods in disorder over it. He greeted random people with attention, without affection, at a distance. His look of impermanence deepened with the autumn.

The city was twilit in the first smokings of the chimneys and the mailboat departing from Captain Bligh's pier acquired a painful nostalgia in the misty dusk, sailing out from Dun Laoghaire, from the orange lights strung like a pulse beating south from the city. The hills of the old monks failed in their attempted starkness, Killiney pointing a needle towards the empty sky. The moon was distrustful that year, behind clouds losing its light reluctantly into the night. The sea at the Forty Foot sucked more hungrily than ever.

The white-haired girl went, rumour said to San Joaquin of Maracon. The Zoo was possessed by flamingoes standing despondently in Liffey water to which had been added pink dye. The otters clowned desperately like gaoled Fenians trying to keep up face. No birds sang at dawn, only the changing couples of the Garda Siochana signalling the hours. The trains pulled in from Howth and Dalkey, running on tracks of reflected sky, and the spiritless bodies of those condemned in their programming spilled out to people the offices with pretence.

He fizzed through the streets now with eyes beginning to splinter into flame. He would explode into a pub or a gathering at a corner or in a flat and the air filled with brittle glass would lose its interest for a moment. He passed through. Everywhere was his comet trail. Everywhere he went he lost things, borrowed things, forgot to return things. Always he was late, always. When he left the coffee shop in the middle of the street one day he left behind a postcard he had meant to send, with a picture of desert with melting watches. Someone passing through put a stamp on it and posted it walking down the street. Fiction so much sweeter than fact, faction so much stronger.

He moved in the streets, a moony gleam in his eyes; through armies of the defeated with passive hands, young girls nubile in globules of I, escaped from convents of sweetness, Honours Arts students, a dream in their eyes looking at the boys from under the make-up, semi-detached, self-contained. The terrible starkness of shop window mannequins gesturing desperately for humanity was echoed in every patent-shod or booted foot that struck the concrete pavements. Vomit and pastels fought in the revolutionary space under the Bank of Ireland; under the G. P. O. Trots and Provies uneasy in Comrade-ship enlightened the workers, safe now from Nelson's one-eyed glare. The roads were desolate.

Yellow roses faded by the dust of passing summer echoed the sunsets over grey streets. Dying was too cumbersome for the survivors who people this barren area, so they continued among the fallen leaves. There was never quite silence

between the painted signs. Ginger men cycled dully through
the fuming lavender and flaming indigo offending bleak skies
in the early sunsets of the evenings of Fall. Sulphurous yellow
fought green reflections, clear and cunning country-shrewd
sky battling the baffling of gurrier clouds piled in corners, a
fag smoking into circled palm. The city snorted.

Women in the streets not blooming in third pregnancy,
humiliated without and within by shrieking gravidity, prams
before them, eyes screaming open; closed, dustcaked
windows of the soul, Venetian-blinded by Catholicism.

Ragbags gathered around bones and bitterness, huddled
around their secrets, secrets dangerous in their keeping as
never in their entity. Dignity is lost in respectability.

The streetwalking coincollectors of Junior Rotary, gathering money for the House of God, clanked their numismatic
oilcans like chains of workers unreleased. Passing, the grey
Murphia of Young Connollies spit at this sop to the bourgeois conscience, but matrons give, and receive the Host
flaglets on to the tongue lapels of wool coats not guaranteed
Irish.

He walked the streets as the leaves yellowed in cancerous
anticipation of rot and regrowth. His tall and hunched figure
floated always somewhere in the distance, magically softening
for any child, exposed against Georgian frontages. The air
was warm and thick, the old danced among the dancing
leaves, ready to fall from the tree of life. Old and young faced
across the barbed-wire barrier of neutral prime. Primes
numerous switched self image from age to youth fickle
muckle or mickle. Alone was always a long never.

He walked springily along Grafton Street, mannequins
thrusting through cotton dresses, winter girls dancey in the
cold sunlight. Bewleys basked (a knot of housewives in waiting) smelling warmly of coffee. The lightful pathway paved an
opening for him, clearing his view, multiple city. Deathy, a
suicide of a year ago stood beside the Liffey, his yellowing

fantastic body and his starlit globe of night not appearing into the daylight of the passers. He stood for year on year, a ticktock stopped layabout derry sleeper of nineteen seventy his last globule of moment preserved in aspic time to trip the unwary tripper on a line of suiciding scream (or was it?). The passer stops, struck in horror by the loneliness of human being. Only always, October forever, and the day again. Stereoscopic afterwards circling to beginning. The city moved in unease.

As the skies and streets softened from city grey to winter grey and the sea ploughed wild with teams of a hundred white horses he was on the mailboat one day alone among a group of rioting musicians, the city behind him, the sea before him.

Photo by Colman Doyle

Francis Stuart was born in Australia of Ulster parents in 1902, and has lived most of his life in Ireland. As a young man, he was considered by W.B. Yeats as one of the great new names in Irish writing. At the age of twenty, he was interned by the Irish Free State for republican activities in the Civil War. He became known as a novelist in the 1930's, and has been a farmer and racehorse owner. He spent the war years in Germany, and later wrote in France and the United Kingdom, returning to Ireland in 1958. He has written some thirty works; his latest novel, 'A Hole in the Head,' was published in 1977. He is a Founder Member of the Irish Academy of Letters. His writing is taught at Trinity College, Dublin.

FRANCIS STUART

The Stormy Petrel

1973

WHEN I CAME back through the hall from cleaning the room assigned to the rabbits, the long white envelope with the foreign-looking crest on the flap lay on the carpet. That's it; yes, my gentle creatures—I was pretending to be communing with the animals rather than have to admit that at such moments I tended to talk to myself—the invitation has come and is safely in my hands.

A pleasant prospect: a dip in a blue-enamelled (was tiled the word I wanted here?) pool before the six-o'clock aperitif, strong, pale, aromatic, followed by dinner on the seaward side, candlelight sparkling on cut-glass decanters (instead of on the cut-price bottle of wine that was my usual weekly treat) and on the sensationally white flesh framed in the V (for Venus) of plunging necklines. For all of which I didn't give an ass's fuck! The real cause of the excitement that was going to my head and making me raise my voice as if addressing the rodents two rooms away was that I could now enact in my imagination the scene in my host's book-lined (when carried away I resort to clichés) study.

How many others among my colleagues had received a similar convocation? Quite a number as it turned out. Many are called but few chosen. Amen to that! Nobody could say later that the net hadn't been spread wide and all the small fry carefully weighed and even in some cases measured before being found wanting; nobody, that is except the cranks and bloody begrudgers.

A train ticket (first class) was clipped to the ambassadorial invitation but from the rail-head there was still a long road to the mansion. Some went by hired car (fare to be defrayed on arrival), two or three started out on foot, hoping, no doubt, to be picked up en route, dusted down, and shown the extra respect accorded those who voluntarily take the lower places. And, if my eyes didn't deceive me (there I go again!), I saw our reverend Arts Councillor perched sideways on the rump of a briskly-trotting jennet.

To vary the style with a touch of the question-and-answer technique: what transport did the central figure select? A bloody boat. Extravagant? All kinds of extravaganzas are fully justified when the stakes are really high: Motto fastened with a safety pin over my four-poster. Seriously though, I needed time to take myself in hand; I, narrator of grim adventures, survivor, if not hero, of bloody, interior battles, had still at this last hour, to prepare myself for what looked like being one of my most difficult private struggles.

The possibility was there, perhaps the probability; I didn't want to follow it that far... not yet. Naturally, it had got round: what the purpose of the house-party was. We all, even the most unlikely candidates for high honour, felt a certain awe, realising that it was a matter of political expediency for the donors this year to choose an aspirant from this blessed land of ours for the *Grand Prix*, triple bar.

What better setting in which to come to myself after the dizzy dreams of the last days than the deck of a small, but sturdy, pitching craft, gripping a rope, the right leg of my jeans, later both, my upper part being shielded by raincoat, salty-soaked?

As soon as the sloop was beyond the headland, off-black swells began overtaking us from a, to me, unexpected quarter and catching us three-quarter beam on. (I have my own nautical style.)

I had to choose one of two possible responses if the... should it happen that... in case the elegant diplomat approached me, drink in hand (*mine*, he was said to be abstemious). First: the one I longed with all my heart to be able to decide on. It would be a matter of adopting a taken-aback, two-parts genuine, one-part phony (with a light sprinking of respectfulness) air, accepting gratefully but preserving a mental loophole so that when the official announcement was made I'd have both the glory and the additional and more select glory of refusing the first glory!

Fantastic! I shivered, not in the watery chill but in the semi-sensual anticipation. Two up and one to play, or, for the non-golfer, bursting out of the ruck with a furlong to cover!

Second (and this would be hard to the point of...leave it, I'm no good at metaphors): tell our immaculately attired host when he laid his hand on the shoulder of my not-so-immaculate (though clean) summer jacket that, while I was overwhelmed, etcetera and so on, it must be a simple No and I prefered that no mention in any media in any country be made of my refusal, as, no doubt, would also suit the illustrious donors. Let the fact that I was declining the piece of pie with the iced sultana at the centre (so it was said, only the recipients actually knew what was there) remain a secret between me and them.

Did I know the right choice for me (this is not a tale about anyone else)? Yes. Was I going to make it? Let's put it like this; was I going to swallow the lollipop, wrapping and all, if I got the chance, before the Committee Chairman had time to let go the ribbon? Yes!

Then it was that the tall, sober-jawed mate at the tiller, who hadn't yet opened his mouth said something that the wind took away before I could catch it.

'Eh?'

A jerk of his head towards the shelter of the hatch that led to the cabin.

'It's O.K.'

Flitting down one of the shadowy valleys overtaking us I

saw this small, black spectre, soon to be the only heart-tick and drop of blood-warmth as the dusk fell on the salt desolation when we were gone.

Omens, warnings, come to those who in their dilemma seek them with a pure heart. But also to those who, no matter how heart-sullied, have the gift of turning make-believe into reality; can make themselves feel and believe what they know is true.

This little fowl of the species that thirst-crazed, ship-wrecked mariners used to call Mother Carey's chickens (as they were transported perhaps to summer evenings at home) was communicating to me in my need: Where I go you will have once to venture, in the chill gales that blow day and night in these parts. Or, again: No impedimenta hung round the neck nor fastened to the wing-tips are anything but fatal in these latitudes.

The sloop slipped into a new pattern-motion; the waves, like a series of too-soft, old brooms that cannot rid a carpet of a splinter except little by little in a succession of sweeps, kept thrusting under the boat and tossing us a little further on.

O, my secret albatross, my marine black-bird with the speck of white (that I first took to be foam) on the rump, and the disproportionately long wings, teach me how not to wait!

For news, for the morning post, for an answer; I must learn to fly just aloft of the storm, but not out of it, to float and ride the wet-ash swells as dawn breaks, head tucked under oily wing.

Who still wants to know the outcome of the story? Anyone who does hasn't bothered to read it.